BE

DEBBIE
MACOMBER

LONESOME
COWBOY

★ HEART OF TEXAS

DEBBIE MACOMBER's

HEART OF TEXAS

PHHRTIFC

Laurie's
Paperback
Exchange

Hilltop Mall
(across from Safeway)
Oregon City
503-655-6586

ISBN 0-373-83342-3

9 780373 833429

50450

Praise for Debbie Macomber and

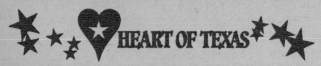 HEART OF TEXAS

"Reading a book by Debbie Macomber reminds me of watching those wonderful Tracy-Hepburn movies with strong lovable characters, quick-paced dialogue and the hard-won happily-ever-after. With Shirley, Goodness and Mercy, Debbie gave us a delightful glimpse of heaven; I can hardly wait to see what she does for Texas."
—Mary Lynn Baxter

"Romance readers everywhere cherish the books of Debbie Macomber."
—Susan Elizabeth Phillips

"Debbie Macomber writes stories as grand as Texas itself."
—Pamela Morsi

"Debbie Macomber writes characters who are as warm and funny as your best friends. She's earned her place as one of today's most beloved authors."
—Susan Wiggs

"Every Debbie Macomber novel is a *don't miss* read."
—Katherine Stone

"Debbie Macomber is one of the few true originals in women's fiction. Her books are filled with warmth and tenderness, full of sweet characterizations that melt the heart and never cloy. Her books are touching and marvelous and not to be missed."
—Anne Stuart

"Debbie Macomber's name on a book is a guarantee of delightful, warmhearted romance."
—Jayne Ann Krentz

"I've never met a Macomber book I didn't love!"
—Linda Lael Miller

Debbie Macomber is one of America's most popular authors. In fact, her appealing characters and heartwarming stories have made her a favorite around the globe.

Debbie has always enjoyed telling stories—first to the children she baby-sat as a young teen and later to her own kids. As a full-time wife and mother and avid romance reader, she dreamed of one day sharing her stories with a wider audience. She sold her first book in 1982—and that was only the beginning!

Today there are more than 40 million copies of her books in print.

Debbie loves to hear from her readers. You can reach her at P.O. Box 1458, Port Orchard, Washington 98366

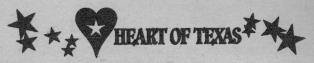

HEART OF TEXAS

Books in order of publication:
Lonesome Cowboy
Texas Two-Step
Caroline's Child
Dr. Texas
Nell's Cowboy
Lone Star Baby

DEBBIE MACOMBER

LONESOME COWBOY

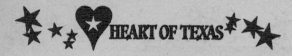

HEART OF TEXAS

Harlequin Books

TORONTO • NEW YORK • LONDON
AMSTERDAM • PARIS • SYDNEY • HAMBURG
STOCKHOLM • ATHENS • TOKYO • MILAN
MADRID • WARSAW • BUDAPEST • AUCKLAND

ISBN 0-373-83342-3

LONESOME COWBOY

Copyright © 1998 by Debbie Macomber

Dearest Friends,

After the success of MIDNIGHT SONS, and those stubborn Alaskan men, Harlequin approached me about doing another six-book series. But where was I going to find heroes to match those strong, endearing bush pilots? The answer wasn't long in coming. I've always had a weakness for cowboys, and no place on earth grows 'em quite like Texas.

So, my friends, here they are: the men and women of Promise, Texas. Situated deep in the Texas hill country, Promise is truly a town with heart, populated by people like you and me— hardworking, proud and just a little sassy. A town with an interesting past and an exciting future.

For the MIDNIGHT SONS series, my husband and I traveled to Alaska. This time around, I conned my editor, Paula Eykelhof, into exploring Texas with me. With a rental car, a map and the sense of direction of a pet rock, Paula and I toured the Texas hill country. We met the people, sampled the barbecues, tasted the wines and gazed endlessly at cowboys. If this wasn't heaven, then we were pretty darn close!

So I invite you to sit back, put your feet up and allow me to introduce you to a few of those Texan cowboys. The men of Alaska started this craziness, but the men in Texas refuse to be outdone. They're just as stubborn, just as ornery, just as proud. And just as lovable.

Enjoy.

Debbie Macomber

THE PEOPLE OF PROMISE:
CAST OF CHARACTERS

Nell Bishop: thirty-something widow with a son, Jeremy, and a daughter, Emma. Her husband died in a tractor accident.

Ruth Bishop: Nell's mother-in-law. Lives with Nell and her two children.

Dovie Boyd: runs an antiques shop and has dated Sheriff Frank Hennessey for ten years

Caroline Daniels: postmistress of Promise

Maggie Daniels: Caroline's five-year-old daughter

Dr. Jane Dickinson: new doctor in Promise

Ellie Frasier: owner of Frasier's Feed Store

Frank Hennessey: local sheriff

Max Jordan: owner of Jordan's Towne & Country

Wade McMillen: preacher of Promise Christian Church

Edwina and Lily Moorhouse: sisters. Retired schoolteachers.

Cal and Glen Patterson: local ranchers. Brothers who ranch together.

Phil and Mary Patterson: parents of Cal and Glen. Operate a local B&B.

Louise Powell: town gossip

Wiley Rogers: sixty-year-old ranch foreman at the Weston ranch

Laredo Smith: wrangler hired by Savannah Weston

Barbara and Melvin Weston: mother and father to Savannah, Grady and Richard. The Westons died six years ago.

Richard Weston: youngest of the Weston siblings

Savannah Weston: Grady and Richard's sister. Cultivates old roses.

Grady Weston: rancher and oldest of the Weston siblings

Chapter One

Grady had warned her repeatedly. He'd told Savannah that the ghost town was dangerous, that it was a disturbing place. He'd told her over and over not to look for it. And all these years Savannah *had* stayed away. But the more her brother cautioned her, the more convinced she'd become that she had to find it. If for no other reason than the roses. Roses were Savannah's passion—especially old roses, planted before 1867 and now found mostly in cemeteries and abandoned homesteads.

It was because of the roses that she ignored Grady's advice and began to seek out the long-lost town.

After a six-week search, roaming about the rugged Texas hill country, first in the truck, then on horseback and finally on foot with no map and little information, she'd located it. Bitter End. What a strange name, but no stranger than the town itself.

No matter how furious Grady was when he discovered what she'd done, it'd been worth the risk. This certainly wouldn't be the first time she'd defied her older brother. Nor would it be the last. Grady seemed to carry the weight of the world on his shoulders; he rarely smiled anymore. He was as loud and demanding as Savannah was quiet and intense. But her stubbornness was easily a match for his.

Glancing at the truck's speedometer, she pressed her foot to the floor, although it generally wasn't in her nature to rush. However, her chances of escaping Grady's anger were greater if she got back to the house before he returned from his duties around the ranch. Not that she *feared* his anger; she simply preferred to avoid it.

Her brother was so often angry these days, with beef prices dropping and all the other problems associated with running a large cattle ranch. It didn't help that, thanks to Richard, they continued to struggle with debt and financial hardship.

Savannah forced her thoughts away from the unhappy events of six years earlier. It was wrenching enough to have lost both parents in one devastating accident, but Savannah feared that their brother's betrayal, which had followed so soon afterward, would forever taint their lives with bitterness.

"Oh, Richard," she whispered as the truck sped down the winding country road. The pain he'd wrought in her life and Grady's was the kind that even love would never completely heal.

Grady had changed in the years since their parents' tragic deaths—and Richard's betrayal. Finances and other concerns had harassed and tormented him until she barely knew him any longer. Through sheer stubbornness and backbreaking work he'd managed to accomplish the impossible. He's saved the Yellow Rose Ranch, but at a terrible price. Grady had sacrificed himself and his youth to hold on to the land that had been settled by their great-great-grandfather shortly after the Civil War. Or, as her Southern grandmother called it, the War of the Northern Aggression.

Savannah had wanted to help with their finances; after all, she had a college education. It would be a small thing to return to school and take the necessary courses to obtain her teaching certificate. The Promise school board had repeatedly advertised for substitute teachers, and a full-time position was bound to become available within a few years. Grady, however, wouldn't hear of it. He needed her on the Yellow Rose, and Savannah accepted that. She handled the majority of the paperwork, cooked, cleaned the house and did the gardening. She'd indulged her love for roses, started keeping goats and occasionally hand-raised orphaned or abandoned calves. For six years she'd picked up the slack and made a decent life for herself. But compared to Grady, she didn't feel she was doing nearly enough.

Her desire to contribute to the family income had prompted her to establish a mail-order business for her roses, and while Grady had politely listened to her plans, he hadn't encouraged them. Her small venture was just now starting to show a profit, of which Savannah was extremely proud. In the past few months she'd been spending her evenings working on a catalog.

What Grady needed, in Savannah's opinion, was to marry and start a family. At thirty-five he was well past the age most men settled into family life. He probably would've done so long before now if he hadn't been required to dedicate every waking minute to the ranch. She wondered whether it was too late, whether he'd ever get married. Savannah herself had long since given up any hope of marriage and children. Her maternal urges would have to be satisfied by her animals, she told herself wryly. She'd turned thirty-one her last birthday and hadn't dated in the past four or five years. She rarely thought about having a relationship anymore. Men didn't understand her quiet ways or appreciate her strength or gentleness of spirit. It no longer mattered. She was content with her life. She'd learned to take pleasure in small things—the beauty of flowers, the affection of animals, the comfort of a well-ordered house.

Indian paintbrush, bluebonnets and pink evening primroses, all in bloom, lined the twisting road. Savannah loved spring. The scent of the air brought with it the promise of warm weather and new life. Grady and Wiley, the hired hand who'd been with them so many years he was more family than foreman, had assisted in delivering fourteen calves this week and were looking for that many more in the next couple of days.

Savannah glanced at her watch and hoped Grady had been delayed this afternoon. Otherwise he was going to have a conniption, especially when he realized where she'd gone.

Sighing, she turned the familiar bend in the road and caught sight of an abandoned truck parked close to the ditch. Savannah didn't recognize the vehicle; that in itself was unusual. People who didn't know the area hardly ever wandered this far off the beaten path.

The truck had seen better days. The color had faded badly and a large dent in the side revealed a section where rust had eaten a hole the size of a small plate. With the truck parked as it was, fifteen miles outside of town, far from anywhere, Savannah couldn't help wondering if something was wrong. She might have stopped to investigate if she hadn't been in a hurry.

The decision was taken from her a few miles down the road when she saw a cowboy walking, carrying a saddle. Even from this distance she could see how weary he was; he seemed to be favoring one side, limping discernibly.

At the sound of her approach, he straightened, shifted the weight of his saddle and stuck out his thumb.

Never in all her life had Savannah stopped for a hitch-hiker, but this man, miles from anywhere and walking in the opposite direction from town, must have been spent.

Savannah pulled over and eased to a stop. She opened the door and climbed out. "Is that your truck parked back there?"

"Yes, ma'am," he answered politely. He was tall and wiry, about her age, she guessed. His Stetson rested low on his brow, shading his face from the afternoon sun. When he touched his fingers to the brim in greeting, she noticed that his eyes were pale blue. "I'd be much obliged for a ride."

Although she'd stopped, Savannah hesitated, unsure what to do. "I wasn't headed toward town."

"As far as you'd take me would be appreciated. Your truck's the first vehicle to come along in more'n two hours." He gave her a tired smile. "I'd hoped to find a ranch and use the phone there, but I haven't seen one yet."

Apparently he didn't realize he was walking away from Promise. "I live ten or so miles down the road." Shielding her eyes from the glare of the sun, she pointed toward the Yellow Rose. Riding with her would only take him farther from where he needed to go. She was about to explain as much, then realized he was tired, hurting and probably hadn't eaten a decent meal in hours, if not days. Grady wouldn't be pleased, but… She shrugged off the prospect of her brother's wrath.

"If you like, you can stay the night in the bunkhouse and I'll drive you to town in the morning."

She could tell that her offer surprised him; his eyes widened briefly. "That's mighty kind of you, ma'am."

The fact that he called her ma'am made her feel dowdy and old-fashioned. She supposed that was exactly what she was, though. No one had to tell her she looked older than her age. She usually wore full-length dresses rather than the more fashionable shirt and jeans; her mother had encouraged this, saying that dresses complimented her tall willowy figure. She'd grown accustomed to working in them, donning an apron for household chores. Her thick straight blond hair fell down her back, almost to her waist. Grady had teasingly called her a flower child of the sixties, and in some ways, she did resemble a hippie.

"I'm Savannah Weston."

"Laredo Smith." Again he touched the brim of his hat.

"Pleased to meet you," she said, and smiled shyly. "Laredo's an unusual name."

He grinned as if the comment was familiar. "So I've heard." He hitched the saddle higher and added, "My given name's Matthew, but when I was a kid and we moved away from Texas, I wanted to take part of it with me. From that day on I only answered to Laredo. After all these years, I don't know who Matthew is, but Laredo...well, it's a comfortable fit and suits me just fine."

Savannah couldn't have said why, but she had the impression that these details weren't something he shared often. She told herself it was silly to feel honored—but she did, anyway.

She must have smiled because he responded with a grin of his own. It amazed her how a simple smile could transform his drained features. A hint of something warm and kind showed in his sun-weathered face, mesmerizing her for a moment. A little shocked by her own response, Savannah decided she was being fanciful and looked away. Laredo Smith was a stranger and she'd do well to take care.

"If you'd like, you can put your saddle in the truck bed," she offered, and walked to the back to lower the tailgate.

The leather creaked as he lifted it from his shoulder and wearily set it down. He hesitated when he saw the roses and reached out a callused hand toward the fragile buds. Gently he fingered a delicate pink petal.

"There are antique roses, aren't they?" He closed his eyes and breathed in the distinctive perfumed scent of the flowers.

His knowledge surprised her. Few people knew about old roses or had heard the term. In her research Savannah had learned that many of the roses found in Texas were of unknown lineage, recovered from hidden corners and byways in an ongoing search-and-rescue mission—like the one she'd been on that very day. Savannah was well aware that some would describe her as a "rose rustler"; it wasn't how she thought of herself. Her overwhelming motivation was her love of the flowers.

"You know about old roses?" she asked.

"My grandmother had a rose garden and she grew roses passed down by her own grandmother. It must be at least twenty years since I saw one. Where'd you ever find these?"

Her pause was long enough for him to notice. "In an old graveyard," she said. "Near, um, an abandoned town." While it was the truth, it wasn't the *entire* truth, but Savannah didn't dare add any details about the ghost town. Only a few people in Promise had even heard of Bitter End. And although Grady had repeatedly warned her against seeking it out, he'd never told her exactly what was so threatening about the long-deserted town.

Only now did Savannah understand her brother's concerns. The dangers weren't found in the crumbling buildings or the abandoned wells; no, they weren't so easily explained. She couldn't help shuddering as she remembered the sensation of...darkness that had come over her when she'd first set foot on the still, silent grounds. Even that didn't adequately describe the emotions she'd experienced. It wasn't a feeling of evil so much as a pressing sadness, a pain and grief so raw that a hundred years hadn't dimmed its intensity.

Knowing little of the town's history, Savannah had felt defenseless and almost afraid. Years earlier, Grady and two of his friends had heard their parents discussing Bitter End, but when Savannah questioned her mother, she'd refused to talk about it. From Grady, Savannah had learned that the town was said to have been settled by Promise's founding fathers. Why they'd moved, what had happened to prompt the relocation, was an unsolved mystery. For all she knew, it was something as mundane as water rights. Although that would hardly account for what she'd felt....

Despite Grady's warnings, Savannah had found Bitter End and dug up the old roses in the graveyard, but she hadn't ventured beyond the fenced area beside the church. She left as quickly as she could. By the time she made it back to the truck, she was pale and trembling.

She'd driven away without looking back. She hadn't investigated any of the other buildings, and she was annoyed now for letting the opportunity pass. She might have found more old roses had she taken the time to search.

"They're beautiful," Laredo said. The light pink bud, perfectly formed, lay like a jewel in the palm of his hand.

"They truly are exquisite, aren't they?" The sheer joy

and excitement she'd felt on discovering the roses quickened her voice. "I just couldn't be happier! It's so much more than I hoped to find!"

His gaze held hers and he nodded, seeming to share her enthusiasm.

Warming to her subject, Savannah added, "It's incredible to think they've survived all these years without anyone to care for them."

Laredo gently withdrew his hand from the rosebud.

"Would you be more comfortable if I rode in the back, ma'am?" he asked.

"Savannah," she insisted.

The smile returned again, briefly. "Savannah," he echoed.

"You're welcome to ride in front with me."

He climbed slowly into the cab and she could see that the action pained him considerably.

"I don't suppose you know anyone who's looking for a good wrangler?" he asked.

"I'm sorry, I don't," she said with sincere regret.

He nodded and winced, pressing his hand against his ribs.

"You've been hurt," she said.

"A cracked rib or two," he answered, obviously embarrassed by her concern. "My own damn fault," he muttered.

"A horse?"

"Not exactly." His voice was rueful, a bit ironic. "I got shoved against a fence by a bull. You'd think that after all these years working ranches, I'd know better than to let myself get cornered by a bull."

"My daddy cracked a rib once and he said it left him feeling like he'd been gnawed by a coyote, then dumped over a cliff."

Laredo chuckled. "Your daddy sounds like he's got quite a sense of humor."

"He did," Savannah agreed softly, starting the engine. She knew the tires hitting the ruts in the road would hurt him, so she drove slowly and carefully.

Laredo glanced over his shoulder—to check on his saddle, Savannah suspected. She was surprised when he mentioned the roses a second time. "I never thought to smell roses like those again."

"I'm so glad I found them!" she burst out. "These are the best ones yet." Their scent was sweet and strong and pure, far more aromatic than modern hybrids. These roses from Bitter End were probably White Lady Banks—a rare and precious find.

Savannah talked excitedly about her roses; the cowboy encouraged her, asking interested and knowledgeable questions.

What surprised Savannah was how comfortable she felt with Laredo Smith. They could have talked for hours. Generally when it came to conversation with a man, especially a stranger, Savannah was shy and reticent. The ease with which she talked to Laredo was unprecedented.

It wasn't just roses they talked about, either. Soon Savannah found herself telling him about her gardens at the ranch and the love her mother, Barbara, had for flowers. One topic led swiftly to another. She described Promise and assured him it was a friendly town. He asked about having his truck repaired and she mentioned a couple of reliable garages.

"Oh, my," she said, and held her palm to her mouth.

"Is something wrong?"

"I got to chatting away and almost missed the turnoff for the ranch." Such a thing had never happened before. Then, hardly knowing what she was doing, she glanced over at him and said, "The fact is, Laredo, the Yellow Rose could use an extra hand. If you need a job, we'd be happy to offer you one."

Laredo brightened visibly. "I'm good with horses and I'm willing to work hard."

"Grady'll probably have a few questions for you." She added this second part knowing her brother wasn't going to be pleased with her hiring a stranger. In the past he'd always been the one to do the hiring and firing, but if he took offense, he could discuss the matter with her. Every instinct she possessed told her Laredo Smith was worthy of their trust. Besides, they needed extra help, whether Grady was willing to admit it or not.

Laredo grew quiet, and then she felt his eyes on her. "Since you offered me the job, I think it's only fair to tell you I was fired from my last position." He told her he'd been accused of theft, wrongly accused. He neither cast nor accepted blame. "I may be a lot of things, but a thief isn't one of them. If you change your mind, I'll understand."

"I won't," she said, but the instincts that had felt so right moments earlier wavered like dry grass whipped by a harsh summer wind. "I...I appreciate your being honest enough to tell me," Savannah said. Naturally the first thing Grady would want from a stranger, especially one *she'd* taken it upon herself to hire, was references. Well—like everything else about this day—she'd cross that bridge when she came to it.

"You won't be disappointed," Laredo added. "You have my word on that."

A plume of dust followed them as they headed down the pitched dirt driveway leading off the highway. No sooner had Savannah pulled into the yard and turned off the engine than Grady dashed out of the barn and stalked toward her like an avenging angel.

"Just where the bloody hell have you been all afternoon?" her brother demanded, ignoring the shambling black dog that trailed him and nudged the fist clenched at his side.

Savannah inhaled deeply and held her breath while she climbed out of the truck. If she hadn't stopped to pick up Laredo, she might have returned before Grady rode in from the range. Rather than answer his questions, she leaned over and scratched Rocket's ears. The old dog, who'd once belonged to their father, was now well past his prime. He wagged his tail in appreciation.

"You might have left a note." Her brother's ranting continued despite her lack of response.

"I apologize, but—" She wasn't allowed to finish.

"I don't want an apology. I want to know where you were all afternoon." His eyes narrowed on the man beside her. "And I have a feeling I'm not going to like the answer."

It mortified her to have her brother yell at her like this in front of Laredo. "Grady," she said urgently, "perhaps we could discuss this inside."

"You did it, didn't you? Even though I warned you! I *told* you not to look for Bitter End! Doesn't anyone listen to me anymore? I thought you were smarter than this! *Anything* could happen to you up in those hills all by yourself. What's the matter with you, anyway? You should know better than to risk your fool neck over something as ridiculous as a stupid rosebush." His face had turned red with anger.

Disregarding Laredo, her brother advanced toward her. Two steps was as close as he got before her newfound friend moved protectively in front of her, directly in Grady's path.

"Who the hell are you?"

"Grady, this is Laredo Smith," Savannah said evenly, praying she sounded calm and in control. "His truck broke down, and, um, I've offered him a job."

A second of shocked silence followed. "You *what?*"

The anger Grady had shown earlier paled in comparison to the fury that blazed in his eyes now. Savannah didn't acknowledge his outburst. "Dinner's in the Crock-Pot. Chili verde, your favorite."

Grady stared at her, his mouth hanging open, as if he didn't recognize her as his sister.

"I'll have everything ready and on the table in ten minutes. Grady, would you be kind enough to show Laredo to the bunkhouse and ask Wiley to wash up?"

"This is Wiley's poker night," Grady muttered. "But I—"

"So it is," she said, and headed up the porch steps and into the kitchen. Her heart pounced like a prairie rabbit's at the approach of a hawk's shadow. "Then there'll just be the three of us."

It didn't take her long to set the table for dinner. When she heard the door swing open, she squared her shoulders, and turned to greet her brother and Laredo with a wide smile. "I hope you two had a chance to introduce yourselves."

"We didn't get around to exchanging pleasantries," Grady snarled.

"Laredo, I hope you'll forgive my brother," she said, placing the warm tortillas on a plate. "It's clear he isn't in one of his more cordial moods."

"Your brother?" The words slipped from Laredo's lips in a low whisper of surprise.

"The two of us are equal partners in the Yellow Rose Ranch," she said as a subtle way of reminding Grady that she'd had every right to hire Laredo.

Still grumbling under his breath, Grady pulled out a chair and reached for the blue-checked napkin.

"Can I help you with anything, Savannah?" Laredo asked, looking around for something to do.

"There's a cold pitcher of lemonade in the refrigerator," she said, hoping Grady realized it wouldn't hurt him any to lend her a hand now and then. She tried not to be judgmental of her brother, but lately he'd grown so cranky and irritable. It was more than their perpetual money problems, she suspected, but whatever plagued him, he kept to himself. Savannah wished he'd be more open with her, share his troubles, but that wasn't Grady's way. Like their father he kept everything locked inside, preferring to carry the burden of his problems alone. Once again she wished he'd think about marriage. She had the perfect woman in mind.

GRADY WESTON was furious with his sister. He didn't know what had come over her. It wasn't like her to openly defy him, nor had he ever known her to pick up a hitchhiker. And never, not once in all these years, had she taken an active role in the management of the ranch. Yet in one single day, his levelheaded younger sister had not only gone against his express orders, she'd gone and hired him additional help. A stranger, no less!

Grady wouldn't have believed it if he hadn't seen it with his own eyes, heard it with his own ears. Savannah wasn't herself. He frowned at Laredo Smith, instinctively distrusting him. One look told Grady the saddle bum was an outsider, a drifter. Not to be trusted. Yet Savannah had invited the man into their home and their lives like a long-lost relative—*and* offered him employment. The problem with Savannah could be reduced to one simple explanation. She couldn't see the bad in people. She was just too damn trusting.

In spite of that, Grady had often admired Savannah for her common sense. But from all appearances, she'd lost every shred of good judgment she'd ever possessed. All within the space of a single day.

"I can't remember when I've tasted better chili," Laredo said, serving himself a second helping when Savannah passed him the bowl.

She lowered her gaze and Grady watched, amazed as color seeped into her cheeks. "I appreciate the compliment, but Nell Bishop's the one who deserves the credit. It's her recipe."

"My compliments to Nell, then, and to you, too."

Savannah's blush deepened. If it wasn't so pathetic, Grady might have rolled his eyes. The town was full of men who were interested in Savannah, but she hadn't given one of them a lick of encouragement. Not a one. *Then she happens on a complete stranger who doesn't look like he's got two dimes to call his own and she practically faints because he compliments her cooking!*

Grady shoved his plate aside, appetite gone. His day had gone poorly. A calf had died after a desperate struggle to save its life, and he wasn't sure the mother was going to make it, either. He'd had the vet out, and they'd done everything they could, but it didn't look promising. If that wasn't bad enough, he'd found a break in the fence line. Luckily he'd been able to repair it before any of the herd had escaped.

The problems never ended. Day in and day out, he faced one crisis after another, each one heaped on top of all the others. He didn't know what it was to laugh anymore, didn't know what it was to spend a night in town drinking with his buddies. Hell, he couldn't even remember the last time he'd kissed a woman. In six years his life had boiled down to two things—work and worry.

It seemed a million years ago that he'd been young and carefree. Everything had changed for him—and for Savannah—in the course of an afternoon. The life he'd lived before they lost their parents was little more than a vague memory.

After a day like this the last thing he needed was for the one constant, the one sane sensible person in his life, to lose her bearings. Go loco on him. Grady glanced at Savannah and he felt his heart twist with sorrow, frustration, guilt. His sister was as lovely as those roses she cared so much about. She was still young and pretty, although she didn't appear to realize that.

Grady hadn't saved the ranch all on his own, nor was he the only one who'd dedicated his life to building back everything they'd lost. He couldn't have done it without her. Savannah had found a hundred ways to encourage him, lighten his load, and he didn't thank her nearly enough.

Regret settled in the pit of his stomach. He shouldn't have laid into her the way he had when she got home, but damn it all, he'd been worried sick. It wasn't like her to disappear and not tell him where she was going. In the past she'd always been conscientious about that, and with good reason.

Even though the risk of her encountering danger was slim, an accident could always happen. It had to his mother and father. Caught in a flash flood, they'd been swept away in a matter of moments and drowned. Never would he forget the day Sheriff Frank Hennessey had come to deliver the tragic news. So it wasn't that Grady didn't trust Savannah, but her disappearance that afternoon had brought back memories he wished he could forget.

But it was more than the memory of his parents' accident that had distressed him. For three or four months now his sister had been asking him about the ghost town. In the beginning he'd answered her questions and hadn't given her curiosity much thought, but when she persisted, he'd asked her a few questions of his own. That was when she mentioned the old roses. Damn fool woman was willing to risk her neck over something as...as unimportant as flowers. If that didn't beat all, he didn't know what did.

Grady had warned her plenty, not that it'd done any good. Hell, he couldn't have found the abandoned frontier town again had he tried. The one and only time he'd ever stepped foot in Bitter End, he'd been about fifteen. Grady and the two Patterson brothers had overheard their parents talking about a ghost town somewhere up in the hills. Without their parents' knowledge the boys had decided to go exploring, to find the place for themselves.

Grady and his friends had set out, thinking it all a grand adventure. As he recalled, they'd spent weeks looking, and when they finally stumbled on the ghost town, it'd spooked them so badly they'd never discussed that day again.

Grady didn't believe in ghosts; he wasn't a superstitious man. But the town was haunted by something he'd been too young to name or understand, something he didn't fully comprehend even now. An unfamiliar sensation had descended on him that day, and not only him, but the others, too. He remembered the silence that had come over them, how they'd whispered to each other as if they were afraid someone could hear. He remembered a feeling of deep sadness and an ambiguous kind of threat. It hadn't made sense then and made even less sense now.

What mattered was his sister, and Grady didn't want her wandering around in the country alone in search of some half-dead flowers. Especially if it meant she was wandering around in Bitter End.

"Would you care for another helping?" Savannah asked Laredo, breaking into Grady's thoughts.

Laredo planted his hands on his stomach and shook his head. "As delicious as it is, I don't think I could manage another mouthful. As I said earlier, this is one of the best meals I've had in years. I hope your brother appreciates what a fine cook you are."

Even from across the table Grady could feel Savannah's pleasure at the other man's remark. It *sounded* genuine, but Grady suspected Laredo Smith was a consummate con man, who knew a good thing when he saw it. It was clear to Grady, if no one else, that Laredo Smith was out to take advantage of his sister. Not that he had a raindrop's chance in hell of doing so as long as Grady lived and breathed. The drifter could sweet-talk some other rancher's sister. He'd get nowhere with Savannah; Grady would personally see to that.

"I'll help with the dishes," Laredo offered.

Grady resisted suggesting that Laredo was laying it on a little thick, but he was already out of Savannah's good graces and she wouldn't appreciate his sarcasm.

"I'll do the dishes later," Savannah said. "It's more important that I take care of the roses."

"I could help you with that," he suggested next, and then, as if qualifying his statement, he added, "My grandmother let me help her."

"That...that would be lovely."

Grady couldn't recall the last time he'd seen his sister this flustered.

Like a schoolboy eager to please his teacher, Laredo stood and carried his empty plate to the sink.

Grady couldn't allow this to continue. It was time he set the other man straight. "Before this goes any further, you need to know, Mr. Smith, that there's no work for you here."

"Excuse me," Savannah said, her voice rising, "but *I* was the one who hired Laredo."

"I'll be happy to drive you back into Promise myself," Grady volunteered, ignoring his sister. "Would *now* be convenient?"

The two men glared at each other.

"Grady," Savannah protested, but to no avail. He'd tuned her out, unwilling to listen to her arguments.

When she couldn't attract his attention, Savannah tried reaching Laredo. She said his name, but he, too, ignored her, eyes locked with Grady's. The silent battle of wills didn't last long. Slowly Laredo's shoulders relaxed, and he nodded. "Now would be fine."

Grady hadn't expected him to capitulate this easily. If anything, he'd anticipated an argument. Laredo Smith was no fool. The way Savannah had fussed over him at dinner, blushed and made a general idiot of herself, there was no telling how much the drifter could take her for.

"I'll get my saddle."

"No!"

Savannah's cry caught them both off guard. Grady's attention flew to her, as did Laredo's.

Her face was red and her hands had tightened into fists. "If you two had listened to me earlier, I could have cleared this up immediately." She exhaled a long shaky breath. "I was the one who hired Laredo."

"And I said I don't need anyone just now," Grady countered brusquely.

"I didn't say I hired him to help you, Grady. Laredo Smith is working for me."

Chapter Two

Laredo sat on the thin mattress and nursed his aching ribs. They hurt a little less now that the aspirin had had time to take effect. Without asking, Savannah had handed him the pills after dinner, as if she knew intuitively how uncomfortable he'd been. She continued to fascinate him, but it was abundantly clear that her big brother wasn't keen on Laredo hanging around her. Not that Laredo blamed him. If Savannah was his sister, he'd keep a close eye on her, too.

Following dinner, they'd transplanted the old roses she'd found that day. Afterward she'd proudly walked him through the flower garden, telling him the names of various plants, describing their characteristics. She grew azaleas, rhododendrons and many others, some of which he'd never seen before. A hedge of sunflowers separated the flowers from a small herb garden. And then there were her roses.

As she led him down the narrow pathways of her rose garden, she stopped to tell him about each one. It was almost, he thought fancifully, as if she were introducing him to her children. Little pieces of her heart, planted and nourished in fertile ground. From the way her roses flourished, she'd obviously lavished them with love and care.

The rows of old roses were what impressed him most—but no less than Savannah's knowledge of their histories. She was able to tell him where each one had come from and when it was first grown. Gesturing in her enthusiasm, she lost her large straw hat; Laredo stooped to pick it up. She smiled as he returned it, but didn't interrupt her history of the Highway 290 Pink Buttons—small roses with double blossoms. Found in this part of Texas, she told him proudly. Her voice was full of reverence as she spoke of the inherent beauty of the old roses, their perfect scent, their ability to survive.

When they'd finished walking around the garden, she wrote out a list of tasks she had in mind for him. Laredo listened carefully, had her show him where he'd find the supplies he'd need and promised to get started first thing in the morning. He was eager to prove she hadn't made a mistake by hiring him, and that her trust in him had been well placed. *Saying* it was one thing, but the proof was in the results.

In the morning, as soon as he finished dealing with his truck, he planned to be in that rose garden working his fool head off. It wasn't wrangling, wasn't what he knew best, but if he treated the roses with the same respect and appreciation he did a good quarter horse, then he'd do fine.

"Cowboy, you got everything you need?" A froggy male voice cut into Laredo's musings, startling him. He swiveled around to find an older man standing just inside the large bunkhouse. Two rows of beds lined the floor—like an army barracks; at the other end was a door leading to the foreman's private room.

"Wiley Rogers," the foreman said.

"Laredo Smith. And yes, thanks, I'm fine for now. I have some stuff in my truck—clothes and such—but I can get those in the morning." He stood and moved toward the man. They exchanged brusque handshakes.

Rogers had to be sixty if he was a day, with legs bowed from too many years in the saddle. "Hear you're workin' for Savannah," he said with a friendly smile.

Laredo nodded.

The foreman chuckled and rubbed his unshaven jaw, eyeing Laredo carefully. Whatever his opinion, he was keeping it to himself. "If that don't beat all," he muttered, still grinning. "Never thought I'd see the day..."

"Beg your pardon?"

"It's nothing," Wiley said. After a moment's reflection he revised his statement. "Actually it *is* something, but you wouldn't understand. Nice meetin' you, Laredo. You need anything else, just give me a holler."

"Thanks, I will." He sat back down on the bed as Wiley retired to his room and closed the door.

Once the lights were out, Laredo lay on his back and stared up at the ceiling, waiting for sleep to claim him. He should've been dead to the world by now. He was exhausted. And for the first time in days the pain in his side had dulled. His belly was full and he had employment, of sorts. He didn't know how long Savannah would find enough tasks to keep him busy, but he didn't imagine this job would last more than a week or two.

As soon as he found out what was wrong with the truck and had it repaired, he'd hit the road. In hindsight, Earl Chesterton had done him a favor by firing him. Although it sure as hell dented his ego to lose that job, especially under those circumstances. His jaw tightened every time he thought about being accused of theft.

But he was determined to look at this as a blessing in

disguise—what his grandmother would have called it. Finding himself unexpectedly jobless was just the incentive he needed to head back to Oklahoma and pursue his dream of breeding and selling quarter horses. After talking about it for years, he was actually going to do it. With the bitterness of being fired from the Triple C Ranch came the sweetness of this chance to live his dream. Even knowing it would mean years of sacrifice, the thought of being his own boss and living on his own land excited Laredo.

Intent on sleeping, he closed his eyes and tried to empty his mind. To his surprise a vivid image of Savannah appeared, clear as anything. He studied her a long while, this warm, gentle woman who'd come so fortuitously into his life. She was a comfortable person, and she possessed a kind heart. He liked Savannah Weston, but then it was impossible *not* to like her. In fact—even more than that—he found himself attracted to her. Strongly attracted.

It was years since a woman had captivated him the way Savannah had. She wasn't like other women he'd known. He'd never felt relaxed or easy around the opposite sex, but Savannah brought out his every protective instinct. She was shy but genuine, and he liked that. He liked that a lot. Pretty, too, without being flashy. He sensed that despite her quiet unassuming manner she had courage and strength. She reminded him a bit of the frontier women he'd read about who'd helped tame the territory of Texas. Especially with those long dresses she wore.

Her brother, on the other hand, was another matter. Hardheaded, stubborn, suspicious. Laredo had taken exception to the way Grady spoke to his sister, but it wasn't his place to get involved in their family affairs.

No, sir.

He'd work here while there was work to be had, get his truck back in good running order, then head for Oklahoma as soon as he could arrange it.

That would be the best thing for everyone. For the Westons and for him.

As SHE'D PLANNED days before, Savannah drove into town the next morning. Her errand list seemed endless. Hardware store, library, the grocery. Finally she was hurrying toward the post office. Her last stop. She realized that the urgency to get back to the ranch had more to do with seeing Laredo again than with any task that waited for her. *Anyone would think you were a schoolgirl!* But she couldn't help the way her heart reacted to the man.

The dinner she planned for that night was Grady's favorite—chicken-fried steak, cream gravy and fresh green beans. A peace offering. He'd barely had a word for her all morning, but then he wasn't communicative at the best of times. Still, there was no mistaking his anger. She'd felt his gaze following her in the kitchen this morning as she'd moved about, preparing breakfast. They'd carefully avoided each other's eyes. Savannah seldom defied her brother, but Grady had left her no option.

Because she'd stood her ground, Laredo was staying. For some reason that made her happier than anything had in years.

Savannah purposely saved the post office till last, hoping Caroline Daniels, the postmistress, would have time to chat. Dovie Boyd, who owned the antique store and the Victorian Tea Room, was just leaving when Savannah pulled into the parking lot. They exchanged cheerful waves.

The interior of the post office was blessedly cool, and

Savannah glanced toward the front counter, relieved to see no other patrons. Deciding to pick up her mail first, she found her post-box key and inserted it into the lock. The metal door swung open to reveal Caroline's nose and brown eyes.

"Is it true?" the postmistress demanded.

"True?" Savannah blinked back her surprise at discovering Caroline's face thrust at her though the small opening.

"I thought I was your best friend."

"You are," Savannah said.

"Then one would think you'd have told me about a handsome stranger working at the Yellow Rose."

Savannah felt color explode in her face. Apparently word of her hiring Laredo had already spread through town. In less than twenty-four hours, too! How, she didn't know—didn't even want to know. This was the problem with living in a small town. Nothing was private. Unnerved, she closed the small door and twisted the key, locking it.

"Savannah!" came Caroline's muffled voice.

Reluctantly Savannah unlocked the box and opened the door. "Who told you?" She withdrew the few envelopes from the box and thrust them into her bag.

"Ellie Frasier, and she said he's cute, too."

"Ellie met him?" Savannah asked. Ellie was the daughter of John Frasier, owner of the feed store. She was young and pretty, and she had a lively, fun-loving personality. More than once Savannah had hoped Grady would notice her, seeing as he made weekly trips to Frasier's for grain and such. Savannah had hinted a couple of times that he needn't rush home—that maybe he could invite Ellie out for coffee or a cold beer. Her suggestions had met with a glare and a low growl that said he didn't take kindly to her matchmaking efforts.

"So, is he as cute as Ellie says?"

Savannah's blush deepened and she raised her hand to her face. "I...I wouldn't know."

Caroline's chuckle was full of disbelief. "Okay, if you won't answer that, then tell me his name."

No harm there. "Laredo Smith."

"So you were able to talk Grady into hiring another hand. Where'd he happen to meet Laredo?"

This was where the story got difficult. "Grady didn't exactly...hire Laredo."

The brown eyes staring at her from the back of her mailbox darkened perceptibly. "What do you mean?"

Savannah sighed. She might as well explain it once and for all and be done with it. "Laredo isn't working for Grady. I'm the one who hired him."

"You?" Those same eyes narrowed. "Meet me up front."

While Savannah had hoped to discuss the events of the day before with Caroline, she'd wanted to bring up the subject of Laredo in her own time. She certainly hadn't expected an inquisition, especially this soon. But lately Caroline had been encouraging her to get out more, mingle. Savannah decided to accept her friend's advice the day Caroline took it herself.

"You've got that look again," Caroline teased when Savannah approached the counter.

"What look?"

"The one that says you're...you know, perturbed."

"Well, I am." As far as Savannah was concerned she had every right to feel perturbed, annoyed and downright peeved. The entire town was discussing her life, or soon would be, particularly when it became common knowledge that Laredo Smith worked for her and not Grady. She absolutely deplored gossip and refused to partake in it. She'd never pry into anyone's personal business. Why, she'd been Caroline's best friend for ages, and not once had she asked who'd fathered five-year-old Maggie. If Caroline felt inclined to tell her, then she would, but Savannah would rather die than ask.

"Get over it, Savannah. It isn't every day a handsome stranger wanders into town."

"Laredo didn't exactly wander into Promise." She supposed she'd have to tell Caroline the truth. That'd be preferable to having her hear wild rumors later on.

"I know. His truck broke down. It's the transmission, and with parts and labor it'll be close to fifteen hundred dollars. Plus it's going to take at least ten days for the parts to come in."

Good grief, Caroline knew more about Laredo than she did! "Who told you all that?" Silly question when the answer was obvious. Wiley had mentioned that he was going to help Laredo tow his truck into Powell's Garage that morning. Paul Powell's wife, Louise, did the paperwork and was a known talker. Apparently she'd been at the garage when Wiley and Laredo arrived. To complicate matters, Wiley tended to have a loose tongue himself. Savannah had the sudden urge to sit down with an entire pitcher of iced tea, only she had the feeling that all the iced tea in the world wasn't going to make anything better.

Caroline watched her closely. In a gentler tone of voice she asked, "You hired him yourself?"

"Yes. I've been looking for someone to help me with the garden and—and now that I'm starting to get more orders for my roses, well, it makes sense to hire some help." She could have managed very well on her own, though, and Caroline knew it.

"You like him, don't you, Savannah?"

"Of course I like Laredo. He's kind and thoughtful and..." She couldn't continue. "Grady was just awful! Oh, Caroline, I was mortified." She brought one hand to her mouth, remembering the confrontation between the two men after dinner.

"Grady? What else is new?"

"I offered Laredo a job. I shouldn't have done it without talking to Grady first, but he needed the work and you know how I've been after Grady to hire an extra hand."

"So *you* hired him, and Grady didn't appreciate your...help."

Savannah looked away. "That's putting it mildly. He insisted he didn't need anyone else and offered to drive Laredo into town that very minute. He made it sound as if he wanted him off our property, the sooner the better. I didn't know Grady could be that rude! I was embarrassed, and angry, so I...I stepped in and claimed I'd hired Laredo to work for me."

Caroline's eyes sparked with approval. "I'll bet Grady just hit the roof."

"Put it this way—he wasn't pleased."

Nibbling on her lower lip, Caroline crossed her arms and leaned against the counter. "So, tell me, how'd you meet your new employee?"

The questions weren't getting any easier. "I saw him walking down the road," Savannah admitted wryly, "and I...I stopped and offered him a lift."

Caroline's eyes widened at this, but she didn't comment. Savannah continued. "He asked about work in the area, and before I could stop myself, I said there was a job on the Yellow Rose.''

"Which is why Grady took an immediate dislike to him," Caroline muttered.

She knew Grady almost as well as Savannah did. "That's right. He acted like a jerk for no reason other than the fact that *I* was the one to hire him. Oh, Caroline, I don't think I've ever been more furious with my brother."

"So what happened next?"

A sense of pride and satisfaction came to her rescue, and Savannah started to giggle. "If only you could've seen Grady's face when I told him Laredo was working for me. I thought he was going to explode." To give him some credit, Grady had kept his mouth shut. Instead he'd stormed out of the house like a two-year-old, leaving Savannah and Laredo standing there in awkward silence.

Caroline burst out laughing. "I can see it all now! Oh, Savannah, I'm so proud of you."

"Really?"

"Really. It's about time someone put Grady Weston in his place. Don't get me wrong, I think the world of him, but he's become such a curmudgeon in the last few years. He takes everything so seriously. I can't remember the last time I heard him laugh."

Savannah's heart went out to her brother. What Caroline said was true, but it was only because Grady carried such a heavy load of responsibilities. In only a few years he'd taken the ranch from the edge of bankruptcy and made it viable again. Finances remained tight, but they were no longer in danger of losing the land that had been in the family for generations. Savannah reminded herself of all this every time Grady's behavior distressed her. And it had never distressed her more than last night. His opinion of Laredo—and by extension, her—was so scath-ing. She knew very well that he considered her "a damned fool"—his favorite epithet—for trusting a stranger.

She lowered her eyes, not wanting Caroline to read her face. "Am I a fool, Caroline?"

"You? You're joking, right?"

"No, please, I need to know. I…I'm attracted to La-redo. I've never felt this way about a man. He's not like anyone else. He listens to me, and even though we've barely met, he…he understands me better than my own brother does. We spent an entire hour in my garden last night, and he let me tell him about my roses. His grand-mother had old roses and he was genuinely interested in what I'm doing."

Caroline's features softened.

"And he's honest. He told me he'd been fired from his last job and why. He didn't have to do that, but he did and I respect him for it." It sounded foolish now, as if everything her brother had said was true.

"What does your heart tell you?" Caroline asked.

Savannah wavered. When she was with Laredo, there was no doubt how she felt, but in the light of cold reality, she was forced to wonder if she really was as gullible and naive as Grady thought. "I'm not sure anymore."

"Why is it so important that you have all the answers right this moment?"

"I don't know, it's just that—"

Caroline laughed. "Be more patient, Savannah. Life has a way of working things out. And for heaven's sake, quit being so hard on yourself! It isn't a sin to be attracted to a man. Why *shouldn't* you be?"

"But…oh, Caroline it's been so long since anyone made me feel this way."

"Then I like him already."

"You do?"

"How could I not? He's brought color to your cheeks."

Embarrassed, Savannah raised both her hands to her face.

"He's made your heart smile."

What a nice way of putting it. That was exactly how she felt.

"And I've never seen you look happier."

She *was* happy, Savannah realized. Deliriously so, simply because a kindhearted man had walked in the garden with her and listened as she told him stories about old roses. He'd more than listened; he'd been interested, asking questions, touching her roses with a gentle hand. Savannah had hardly slept the entire night, thinking about their time together.

"I'm too old," she blurted. Of her entire high school graduating class, she was the only one still unmarried. Two were already on their second marriages, Savannah hadn't even managed to fall in love.

"Nonsense! Too old?" Caroline countered. "That's the most ridiculous thing you've ever said."

"Ellie's right—Laredo *is* handsome. Why would he be interested in someone like me?"

"Because you're beautiful, Savannah, inside and out. He'd be a fool not to recognize that. Now stop worrying and just be yourself."

Savannah felt only slightly reassured. Her biggest fear was that she'd made more of this attraction than there was. She'd barely known Laredo twenty-four hours, and yet it felt as if she'd known him all her life. She was afraid this might be some unrealistic fantasy. It didn't seem possible that he could share her feelings.

"Can you still watch Maggie on Monday night?" Caroline asked hopefully, interrupting Savannah's relentless worries.

"Of course," Savannah told her. She enjoyed having the five-year-old over while Caroline did volunteer work as a math tutor. Grady intimidated the little girl, but Maggie was slowly warming to him, and although Grady wasn't admitting it, he'd come to enjoy Maggie's visits, as well.

"When I drop her off, I can meet your Laredo for myself."

Your Laredo. Savannah blushed and smiled. "He might not be there."

"Then I'm going to plant myself in the living room until he shows up. I'm dying to meet this marvel who's made my very dearest friend finally—*finally*—fall for a man."

"I was thinking of asking him to come to church with me on Sunday," Savannah said. Actually the idea had just occurred to her, and she looked to Caroline for confirmation of its worth.

"Great! I can meet him then. And so can everyone else."

Everyone else. Savannah's heart fell. Tongues were sure to wag if she showed up at Sunday services with a man on her arm. Well, let them, she decided suddenly. She'd speak to him about church this very afternoon.

"I DON'T WANT to talk about it," Grady growled at Wiley as they rode back toward the ranch house that afternoon. They'd spent most of the day searching through brush for cows and newborn calves. He was completely drained, mentally and physically. Grady had been up late every night for three weeks, checking on newborn calves in the calving barn. Sleep this time of year was a luxury for any rancher.

Wiley looked offended. "Hey, I didn't say a word."

"That may be, but you're about ready to burst with curiosity, I can tell."

"Seems to me you're wantin' to say your piece, otherwise you wouldn't't've mentioned it."

It being Savannah and the hand she'd hired. Even now Grady couldn't believe what she'd done. He had trouble grasping the fact that his own sister could behave like a dithering fool over some saddle bum.

But he'd had an even harder time accepting what Richard had done. It'd taken weeks for everything to sink in, and even then, Grady couldn't understand how his own brother could betray them. Only when the bills piled up and the federal government had come after the inheritance tax had he been forced to face the truth. Richard was a bastard, pure and simple. As for Smith...

"I don't like him," Grady announced. That was all he intended to say. If Wiley commented, fine. If he didn't, that was fine, too.

"You talkin' about Laredo Smith?"

"Smith," Grady repeated with a snicker. "Mighty convenient surname if you ask me."

"Lots of people called Smith."

"My point exactly," Grady snarled. As a rule Wiley wasn't this obtuse. "I'd bet my snakeskin boots the name's phony."

"He seems like a fine young man to me."

It didn't set well that his friend, his confidant, his foreman would take the other man's side. "What do you mean?"

"He's a real worker. He was up early, wanting to get started in Savannah's garden before I helped tow his truck into town. We had it to Powell's by the time they opened, and Paul took a look at it while we were still there."

"What's wrong with it?" Grady had decided he wanted nothing to do with this hired hand of Savannah's but it was in the best interests of his family to learn what he could.

"Transmission needs to be replaced and the brakes are shot, too. Paul said once he got the parts, he'd have it running in a couple of days."

"Good." Grady suspected the stranger would disappear about the time his truck was repaired.

"He doesn't look like he's got cash enough to pay for it once the work's done."

"What?" Grady groaned.

"You heard me. Why else do you think he was lookin' for a job?"

They headed toward the creek and slipped out of their saddles to allow their horses a long drink of cool water. Grady didn't like the idea of Laredo lingering at the Yellow Rose. He'd seen men like Smith before. Drifters, washed-up rodeo riders, shiftless men with shiftless lives. No roots or families. They spent their money as fast as they earned it without a thought to their next meal, let alone the future. They might work hard, but they also played hard and lived harder. Laredo Smith wasn't the type of man he wanted hanging around his sister, that was for damn sure.

"Find out anything else about him?" Grady asked, kicking a rock with the toe of his boot. His interest was out in the open now, no reason to hide it.

Not waiting for Wiley's reply, Grady climbed back into the saddle with the ease of a man long accustomed to riding.

"I thought you said you didn't want to talk about it."

Grady tossed his foreman a furious look, but Wiley responded with a knowing chuckle. The old man knew he could get away with saying what he damn well pleased, and an angry glower wouldn't change that.

"He let drop a few bits of information on the way into town," Wiley admitted as he, too, remounted. "He's been workin' on the Triple C over in Williamsburg for the last couple years."

Grady had heard of the ranch, which was one of the larger spreads in the Texas hill country. He'd spoken to Earl Chesterton, the owner, a time or two at the district cattlemen meetings, but they were little more than nodding acquaintances. Compared to the Triple C, the Yellow Rose was small stuff.

"You gonna check on him?" Wiley asked in a tone that said he disapproved of the idea.

Grady snorted. "Why would I do something like that? He doesn't work for me, remember?"

"You're the one with all the questions," Wiley pointed out.

"I was curious. You can't blame me for that, especially when all I'm doing is looking out for Savannah." He didn't want to say it out loud, but he was worried about his younger sister. Not once in all these years had she openly crossed him. Not that she didn't have any opinions, and not that she was meek or passive, like some people assumed.

Savannah had ways of making her wishes known. Subtle ways. The fact was, he'd come to recognize that when she baked his favorite peach cobbler, she had something on her mind. She'd wait until after dinner; when he was enjoying dessert, she'd sit down with him, sweetness personified, and ask a few harmless—but pertinent—questions. Slowly she'd lead up to what she really wanted, making her point casually and without fanfare.

Grady always listened, and often her nonconfrontational style worked and he'd change his mind. He considered himself a fair man; if he felt her concern was valid, he acted on it.

Then Laredo Smith arrived, and suddenly his sister's behavior had undergone a drastic change. She'd actually raised her voice to him, and all because of this worthless drifter. Well, she was welcome to Laredo Smith. If she wanted to walk around with her heart dangling from her sleeve, acting like a lovelorn fifteen-year-old, he wasn't going to stop her. By the same token, he wouldn't offer sympathy when a month or two down the road Laredo left her high and dry.

"How old is Savannah now?" Wiley asked. "She's over twenty-one, right?"

"You know damn well how old she is."

Wiley set his Stetson farther back on his head and grinned. "You're right, I do. I was just wondering if *you* did."

Grady frowned. "She's old enough to know better."

"Old enough to know her own heart, too, I'd say."

Grady nudged his gelding, Starlight, into a trot and turned toward the house, following the fence line. He wanted to check that it was secure and ascertain the condition of the windmill and water tank before he headed in for the night.

"Like I said earlier," he announced stiffly, "I don't want to talk about it."

"Then you aren't interested in hearin' what else Smith said."

What Grady wasn't interested in was playing games. He reined in Starlight and turned to look back at the foreman. "You got something to say, then I suggest you say it."

"He's a wrangler."

Grady wasn't impressed. Wranglers were a dime a dozen in Texas.

"We could use a good wrangler. Payin' someone to come in and care for the horses can get downright costly."

"I can take care of them myself."

"Sure, the same way you can deliver calves, plant alfalfa, move herds and everything else all by your lonesome. Hey," he said with a shrug, "it was just a suggestion."

Despite his dour mood, Grady threw back his head and laughed. "Wiley, why do you think I'm paying you the big bucks? Since you're so concerned about my welfare, *you* can be my wrangler from now on. You think we need to take one on full-time? Then I'm naming you the Yellow Rose's official wrangler. You can feed, water, groom and worm the horses from this day forward. Don't forget to take care of the tack, too, while you're at it."

"Quit foolin' around."

"Do I look like I'm fooling?" Grady asked with a broad grin. The expression on Wiley's face was worth a thousand bucks. For the first time in longer than he cared to remember, Grady threw back his head and laughed until his throat felt raw.

SAVANNAH SET THE PLATTER of chicken-fried steak on the oven rack and turned the saucepan of thick cream gravy to simmer. The green beans were tender, and she'd sliced fresh tomatoes from her kitchen garden. An apple pie cooled on the counter. All she needed to do now was stir up a pitcher of lemonade, and dinner would be ready when Grady and Wiley returned.

With a few extra moments on her hands, she decided to step outside. Laredo had been working all afternoon in the hot sun, and knowing he was probably thirsty, she poured him a glass of iced tea. As she walked into the sunshine, she was honest enough to admit that the tea was only an excuse to be with him.

Her gardens had never looked better, but she couldn't find Laredo. He'd been there no more than five minutes ago. Disappointed, she was about to return to the house when she spotted him in the goat pen with Samson and Delilah, her two kids. They were a thank-you gift for the roses she'd given a friend for an anniversary party. Seeing Laredo, she felt her heart go still, and she smiled with pleasure.

Grady had delighted in teasing her about her pets. He called it a silly woman thing, viewing her goats the same way he did her roses. He didn't care one whit about something she dearly loved. Roses were her heart, her joy, her passion. Sometimes Savannah wondered if they could truly be brother and sister, their differences seemed so profound.

Laredo knelt in the grass with the two young goats, petting them, talking to them. Samson, in particular, didn't normally take to strangers, but apparently Laredo was a special case.

Savannah wasn't sure how long she stood there watching. Several minutes, anyway, because the cold glass in her hand had numbed her fingers. Not wanting Laredo to know she'd been spying on him, she returned to the house. She set the glass aside and raised her cold hands to her face, to cool her flushed cheeks.

Incredibly the urge to cry came over her, and she

didn't know why. She'd barely exchanged a word with Laredo all day; they'd both been busy with their own chores. And yet Savannah had never felt closer to anyone than she did to him for those few moments, watching him with her goats.

This stranger, this man she barely knew, possessed the ability to touch her soul. Savannah wondered if she'd ever be the same.

Chapter Three

Savannah enjoyed listening to Wade McMillen preach. His messages, simple and direct, cut straight to the heart. He was the most unlikely preacher she'd ever seen. A large man, tall and muscular, he looked as though he'd be more comfortable at home herding cattle than delivering sermons. Perhaps that was what made him so popular.

It might have been her imagination, but Savannah felt the curious stares of those around her. The word about her and Laredo was out, she was sure of it. Now everyone in the town knew she—and not Grady—had hired him.

Soon she'd be the subject of speculative comments and whispered questions—if she wasn't already. She felt mortified, but pride helped her hold her head high and look straight ahead. Her mind wandered throughout Wade's sermon, though, something that didn't usually happen. When her thoughts weren't focused on the consequences of her actions, they zoomed with startling ease to Laredo.

She'd wanted to invite him to church and had tried to broach the subject a number of times, but had lost her nerve. Even an invitation to Sunday-morning worship had seemed rather brash. In light of the interest she'd generated, Savannah would be forever grateful that Laredo *wasn't* with her. His presence would've set tongues wagging for sure.

Laredo had worked all day Saturday building trellises, even though she'd insisted she didn't require him to work weekends. He'd brushed aside her protests and pounded and sawed from dawn to dusk. By the end of the day, a long row of freshly painted trellises stood drying in the late March sun.

After dinner he sat on the porch with her until Grady arrived. Her brother's disapproval was evident in everything he said and did. She wanted to plead with Laredo to ignore him, wanted to insist she was her own woman, but again she remained silent.

A coward, that was what she was. Savannah would've given just about anything to find the courage to tell him what was on her mind and in her heart.

Actually, as Caroline had said, she'd done one thing that made her proud. She'd stood up to Grady, and because she had, Laredo was still at the ranch. Challenging Grady was no easy task. His strong personality had quelled braver souls than hers.

The congregation stood, and Savannah reached for the hymnal and opened it to the appropriate page. Her soft voice lifted with those in the choir. She glanced over at Caroline, standing in the front row of the choir in her long white robe. Her friend must have noticed because she acknowledged Savannah with an almost imperceptible wink. Savannah relaxed for the first time since she'd entered the church that morning.

After a closing prayer organ music once again filled the church and the service ended.

Savannah followed Nell Bishop and her two children out of the pew. Jake Bishop had been killed in a freak tractor accident three and a half years ago. They'd always seemed the perfect couple, so deeply in love—a great team, everyone said. Savannah knew life had been difficult for Nell without Jake and she admired the other woman's strength. Nell had refused to leave the ranch, working it herself. When asked why she hadn't sold off the spread and moved into town, Nell had simply explained that keeping the ranch was what Jake would have wanted. Walking with Nell, Savannah felt safe from gossip. The widow was a private person, as she was herself, and would never pry into her affairs.

Louise Powell stood in the vestibule, craning her neck. Savannah strongly suspected the woman wanted to grill her about Laredo.

Savannah wished there was some way she could just vanish.

"Savannah! Savannah, over here!" Louise raised one gloved hand and waved frantically.

It would do no good to avoid her, Savannah decided miserably. If there was one thing she hated more than gossip, it was being the center of attention.

As soon as she reached the vestibule, Louise was at her side. Louise had celebrated her fiftieth birthday in January and hated the thought of being a half a century old. In the weeks since, she'd changed her hairstyle and purchased a new wardrobe, trying for a younger look. Unfortunately she came across as a woman who was obviously fifty and dressed like twenty-five.

"I met your new friend!" Louise exclaimed. Savannah suspected this was Tammy Lee's influence on her. Tammy Lee—Louise's new friend—was a middle-aged divorcée whose reputation could charitably be described as colorful. "What a nice young man." She paused, waiting for Savannah's comment, but when none was forthcoming, she plowed ahead, wrapping her arm around Savannah's waist. "I understand he's working for you." An annoying giggle followed. "Savannah, I wonder if we really know you, after all. I've always thought of you as shy and retiring, but you know what they say about still waters." The girlish giggle returned.

"There's someone I have to see," Savannah said in an effort to escape.

"Laredo?" Louise asked. This was accompanied with a squeeze tight enough to make Savannah wince. "If you run out of work for him, you send him my way, understand?"

"If you'll excuse me, please..." Savannah said a little desperately.

The Moorhouse sisters, Edwina and Lily, stepped into the vestibule, distracting Louise. Both were retired schoolteachers. Miss Edwina had been Savannah's first-grade teacher and Miss Lily her third. The two were inseparable and Savannah loved them dearly.

"Good morning," Savannah mumbled as she slipped past the elderly pair.

By the time she walked outside, she felt like gasping for air. Reverend McMillen stood just outside the large double doors and greeted each parishioner by name. Wade had a way of looking at a person and seeing more than the obvious. "Are you okay, Savannah?" he asked, holding her hand between both of his. "You're looking flushed."

"I'm fine. Just a little warm." Her discomfort had more to do with attracting unwelcome attention. All she wanted was to hurry home before someone else had the chance to corner her.

"Savannah! Savannah!" Maggie Daniels, Caroline's five-year-old daughter, raced to her side and proudly offered her a crayon drawing she'd made in Sunday-school class.

"Hi there, Maggie-may. What's this?" Savannah asked, studying the paper. Maggie was her joy, the child of her heart. It had been a shock when Caroline Daniels announced she was pregnant her senior year in college. From the beginning there'd been plenty of speculation about the father of Caroline's child, but Caroline had never said, and no one had ever asked. Caroline's mother, Florence, had served as postmistress in Promise for years, and when she died last spring, Caroline had taken over her duties.

Maggie had apparently transferred her love for her grandmother to Savannah. It made Savannah feel privileged, and she reciprocated the child's feelings a hundred percent. Recently Caroline had relied more and more on Savannah to baby-sit, but she never minded. It was a delight to spend time with the little girl.

"That's Joseph," Maggie explained now, pointing to a lumpish figure in her drawing.

"Ah, I see," Savannah said. "He's wearing his coat of many colors. Look what a good job you've done!"

Maggie glowed with pleasure. She tucked her small hand in Savannah's. "Where's Mommy?"

Savannah was about to ask the same thing. The question was answered soon enough when Caroline exited the side door with the other members of the choir. It generally took her a few moments to hang up her robe and put away the music sheets.

"Mommy, Mommy, look!" Maggie cried, rushing toward her mother, pigtails bouncing. The youngster threw her arms around Caroline as if it'd been a year since they'd seen each other.

"Would you like to join us for brunch?" Caroline asked, lifting Maggie into her arms.

Savannah declined with a quick shake of her head. "I put a roast in the oven before I left."

"Did Louise corner you?" Caroline lowered her voice.

"She tried."

"Hey, give the old biddy something to talk about."

"Caroline!"

"She's jealous, that's all."

"Jealous of what?" Savannah wanted to know.

"Of you. For being young and pretty and having a good-looking man in your life."

"Laredo's not in my life—at least not in the personal sense," Savannah felt obliged to protest—although she wished it wasn't true. She'd like him to kiss her or hold her hand—anything so she'd know he felt the same things she did. Once she'd caught him looking at her and she thought he seemed...interested, but she couldn't be sure. If she'd had more experience, she'd know.

"Well, more's the pity," Caroline said with a laugh. "A little romance would do you a world of good."

"What about you?" Caroline was a fine one to talk. Savannah couldn't remember the last time her friend had gone out on a date.

"Me? Romance?" Caroline shook her head. "No, thanks. I've had enough romance to last me a lifetime."

"Oh, Caroline, don't allow one negative experience to sour you forever."

Sadness dimmed her eyes, although Caroline made an effort to hide it. "Some people are meant to fall in love, and then there are people like me..." Her words faded and she looked away.

Savannah's heart went out to her, but she didn't know what else to say.

LAREDO HEARD Wiley whistling in the back of the bunkhouse. The old coot was certainly in a good mood. By nature the foreman appeared to be an easygoing sort, but this afternoon he was downright cheerful.

Stitching a stirrup, Laredo inserted the needle into the worn leather. No one had asked him to repair the saddle, but he had time on his hands, and keeping himself occupied was better than sitting around doing nothing. He wasn't a man who could remain idle long.

Although it was none of his concern, he'd visited the barn and inspected the horses. They were well cared for and in good health. Widowmaker, the stallion kept for breeding purposes, reminded Laredo of Grady. Man and beast shared the same temperament—although he figured he'd have a better relationship with Widowmaker than he ever would with Grady. Horses instinctively recognized Laredo as a friend. He shared an affinity with them that was the key to his success as a wrangler. From the time he was a toddler he'd enjoyed working with his father and their horses.

One of his fondest childhood memories was of his father holding him high enough to pet and talk to Midnight, a beautiful roan gelding. Memories of his father were few and far between. Laredo had been six when word came that Russell Aaron Smith had been killed in a country with a name he couldn't pronounce. He'd bled to death in a rice field six thousand miles from home. Shortly afterward Laredo's mother had moved back with her parents, into the very house where she'd been born, and had never remarried. His grandfather was a good man, patient and caring, but he'd owned an office-supply store and didn't understand Laredo's love of the country or his passion for horses.

As a teenager Laredo had started working summers on

local ranches. His talent was soon recognized. To please his mother he'd graduated from high school, but the instant that diploma had been placed in his hand he was gone. She'd dated Clyde Schneider for years and Laredo had always assumed that once he was out of the picture they'd finally get married, but it hadn't happened.

His mother would love Savannah, Laredo thought, but he hesitated to say anything in his next letter home for fear she'd give the relationship more importance than it warranted. Laura Smith wanted grandchildren and brought up the subject at every opportunity, reminding him that it was time he settled down, started a family. He'd dismissed her heavy hints; he didn't consider himself the marrying kind. Not now, anyway, when he had nothing to offer a woman other than a few hundred dusty acres he'd bought in Oklahoma and a stallion he'd recently spent his life savings to acquire. Laredo was on his way to pick him up. Renegade—the horse he'd pinned his dreams on. The horse he hoped would sire a dynasty of quarter horses. But right now that was all he had—and Savannah Weston deserved a damn sight more. If he was ever in a position to entertain marriage, he hoped he found a woman like her. No, he couldn't mention Savannah to his mother; if he did he'd never hear the end of it.

Wiley broke into song and Laredo gave an involuntary shudder at the off-key rendition of an old Kenny Rogers hit. He couldn't recall the title, but it was some ballad about a woman not taking her love to town. In Wiley's version the words were barely distinguishable, the tune not at all.

When Wiley appeared, his hair was wet and slicked back, his boots polished. He wore a tan suede jacket and string tie with a turquoise piece the size of a silver dollar. He reeked of cologne so strong, Laredo's eyes watered.

"You're lookin' right pretty," Laredo teased the foreman.

Wiley laughed. "I'm off to visit the Widow Johnson in Brewster. Grady can work himself into an early grave if he wants, but I've got places to go, people to see. Don't be concerned if I'm a bit late this evening." He winked and all but danced out the door.

If Laredo remembered correctly, Brewster was at least a hundred miles east of Promise. Wiley's cheer was contagious, though, and he couldn't keep from smiling at the older man's pleasure. His task finished, Laredo carried the saddle back into the barn and returned his tools. He'd watched Savannah walk out to the car this morning, a Bible in her hand, and knew she was headed for church.

He couldn't remember the last time he'd darkened the door of a house of worship.

As twelve-thirty approached he found himself listening and watching for Savannah. He would have enjoyed spending more time with her, but her watchdog of a brother made that difficult. Every time they were alone for more than a few minutes, Grady showed up. Rather than place Savannah in the awkward position of having to defend her actions, widening the rift that already existed between brother and sister, Laredo made his excuses and left. He'd dined with them only once, the night of his arrival, preferring to eat with Wiley in the bunkhouse ever since.

When he left the barn, Laredo saw the car, which meant Savannah was back. He must have stood in the same spot for five minutes trying to decide what to do. Grady was out checking the herd, so he'd probably be away for several hours. This was the perfect opportunity to seek out Savannah's company. A tempting thought.

On the other hand he wasn't doing her any favors by leading her on. He had nothing to offer her other than a few stolen kisses. Besides, he'd already decided that, once he'd earned enough to pay for the truck repairs, he'd be on his way. And yet...

He shook his head. He barely knew the woman, and even if a relationship developed between them, it would do no good. He'd be living in a small secondhand trailer while he built his business from the ground up. It'd be years of blood and sweat before he had anything to show for his efforts. One day in the distant future his stock would be legendary; he was certain of it. But until then...

When he left Promise, he wanted to go without regrets. Savannah was sweet and gentle, and he'd rather cut off his right arm than hurt her. He wasn't stupid; he saw the look in her eyes. Even though she tried to hide it, she was interested. Damn it all, so was he!

She was the type of woman a man introduced to his mother. Savannah deserved more than a flirtation. He should go back to the bunkhouse now before he started something he couldn't stop. Something he had no *right* to start.

The decision was taken from him when Savannah stepped onto the back porch. When she saw him standing there, staring at the house like...like a stunned steer, she paused. A look of pure joy lit up her face.

"I was just about to ask you to join me for lunch," she said.

He knew he should politely decline, but he hadn't the heart to disappoint her—or deny himself the pleasure of her company. "I'll wash up and be inside in a minute."

On his way toward the house he started whistling;

when he realized what he was doing, he stopped. He shouldn't be this happy. Damn it all, he was looking at trouble with his eyes wide open and grinning like a schoolboy.

The scent of roast beef greeted him as soon as he entered the kitchen. Savannah was bent over the stove, pulling a tray of biscuits from the oven. The scene was a homey one. After years of meals on the run, it was a rare treat to sit down at a real table, to have lunch with a woman, to eat in a civilized and leisurely fashion.

"When did you have time to make those?" he asked. She couldn't have been home more than ten minutes.

"Early this morning," she said, scooping the biscuits from the tray and placing them in a breadbasket. Everything else was already on the table.

He seated her and bowed his head while she said grace, then reached for a biscuit. It was too hot to hold, and he tossed it between his hands, making Savannah laugh. A man could get used to hearing this woman's laugh, he mused. Warning signs flashed in every direction, and again Laredo ignored them.

"They're buttermilk biscuits," she said. "The recipe was my mother's." She waited for him to take his first bite.

The biscuit was incredible. The best he'd ever tasted. He told her so and watched her eyes light up at the compliment.

"It'll just be the two of us. Grady's busy just now." She didn't meet his eyes.

Laredo already knew as much. "Would you rather I ate in the bunkhouse?" he asked.

"Oh, no! I like being with you."

"Me, too." He supposed he shouldn't tell her that but found it impossible to keep to himself.

Savannah started passing him serving dishes. "How was your morning?" she asked, handing him the platter of sliced roast beef.

He wanted to tell her he'd missed her; instead, he helped himself to the carrots and potatoes. "I wrote a couple of letters," he said as he set the bowl aside.

Their conversation felt stilted and awkward in the beginning, as if they were unsure of each other, afraid of saying too much or too little. But gradually he grew comfortable speaking with her again. There was a naturalness about Savannah. When she asked him questions, her interest was so obviously sincere that he couldn't help responding with equal sincerity.

Following the meal, they sat and lingered over coffee. Savannah asked about his family and perhaps because he'd written to his mother earlier, he described his early years in Texas before his father had gone off to war.

She was such a good listener that Laredo continued, recounting his father's death and the move to Oklahoma to live with his mother's parents, both dead now. He told it all as casually as if he was discussing the weather. In an unemotional voice, he talked about the painful details of those early unhappy years, things he'd rarely shared with anyone.

He sensed that Savannah intuitively understood the significance of the memories he confided in her. She understood and appreciated that he was sharing a piece of his soul, although he made light of it, even joked. But he suspected that the pain revealed itself in the pauses, the unspoken words, and that she was attuned to it.

Her questions were thoughtful and perceptive. After a time he thought he should reciprocate. "What about you, Savannah?" he asked. "Tell me about your family."

She left the table so fast he wondered if his question

had offended her. She stood with her back to him, supporting herself on the kitchen counter. He longed to place his hand on her shoulders. Apologize.

He of all people should know enough to respect the privacy of another's pain. After talking about himself nonstop for more than an hour, with her constant encouragement, he'd felt a certain right to ask. It was a right he didn't have. Savannah owed him nothing. Nothing. He was the one in her debt.

"Savannah, I'm sorry," he whispered. He raised his hands to touch her and dropped them just as quickly.

She was still turned away from him, her head still lowered. "Did you know I have two brothers? Grady and Richard."

"No, I didn't know that."

"Richard's younger than me. He's twenty-nine." She turned then, to face him.

"Does he live close by?" he asked gently.

She shook her head. "I don't know where he is. Neither Grady nor I have seen Richard in six years—since the day we buried Mom and Dad."

Laredo didn't know how to respond. He continued to fight the urge to put his arms around her and found it more and more difficult to resist. Speaking of her younger brother clearly upset her.

"He...disappeared." Her voice was shaking with emotion.

"Savannah, listen, you don't need to say any more. I shouldn't have asked." Her pain was right there, and so real it was agony to see. He felt helpless, unable to console her.

"No...please, I want to tell you."

He nodded.

She took a moment to compose herself. "Apparently

Dad told Grady that if anything were ever to happen to him, Grady should go to the safe-deposit box at the bank in Brewster.'' She paused and bit her lower lip. ''The day before the funeral Grady and Richard visited the bank together. You can imagine how shocked they were to discover that the safe-deposit box was full of cash. Grady estimated there must have been close to forty thousand dollars there, along with a letter.

''Dad wrote that he'd seen what had happened to people who put their faith in life-insurance companies and after the savings-and-loan fiasco, he didn't trust banks much, either. He didn't want Mom and us three kids to worry about finances, so he'd been putting the money aside little by little for years. His plan was that there'd be enough money to pay the inheritance taxes on the ranch, plus keep the place going. I don't even think my mother knew.

''The next day we buried my parents,'' Savannah whispered, and her voice quavered with remembered pain. ''I recall almost nothing about that day. Again and again I've gone over the details in my mind and it's all a blank. I remember the people—so many friends and family came. I remember how kind and generous everyone was. That part I have no problem with. What I can't recall is the last time I saw Richard. He vanished without a word to anyone. At…at first we assumed that something terrible had happened to him. That in his pain and grief he'd done something crazy. I was worried sick. Grady, too.''

Slowly Savannah raised her eyes and Laredo could see that they'd filled with tears. When she spoke again, her voice was small and weak. ''He took the money—every dime. As best as we can figure, he left the funeral and went straight to the bank, forged Grady's signature and cleaned out the safe-deposit box. He took what belonged to all three of us. He left us with nothing. We'd just lost Mom and Dad. Our grief was unbearable, and he made it worse with his betrayal. Neither Grady nor I have heard from him since.'' Some of her tears spilled over. "Grady's never been the same. He's practically killed himself trying to hold on to the ranch, and I think he hates Richard.

"I can't hate him—he's my brother. You see, Laredo, in one day I lost my parents, and I lost both my brothers, too.''

Nothing could have kept Laredo from reaching for her then. When he did, she came to him as though he'd held her a thousand times. It felt so...*right* to press her against his heart. Her body was warm and pliant, molding to his as naturally as if they'd been designed for each other.

Laredo had no idea how long they stood there. Not nearly long enough, of that he was sure. Savannah's arms were around his middle, her face buried in his chest. His hands were in her hair, his eyes closed, savoring the wonder of being close to someone this beautiful and this good.

He didn't hear the door open, but he should have realized it was bound to happen.

The screen door slammed and Laredo's eyes shot open. Instinctively his arms tightened around Savannah before he reluctantly released her and faced her brother. Eye to eye. Man to man.

"What the hell do you think you're doing with my sister?'' Grady Weston shouted.

GRADY MULLED OVER what he had to say before he confronted Savannah. Pacing the living room floor, he carefully weighed each word.

Okay, so maybe he'd been out of line earlier when he found her and Smith clinging to each other like lovers. The sight had distressed him and before he could stop himself he'd exploded.

He didn't want to fight with Savannah. She was his sister, but damn it all! Her infatuation with Laredo Smith—or whatever his name might be—had deprived her of all reason. It was more than he could bear, watching her make a fool of herself over this useless drifter.

Unfortunately his methods of convincing her hadn't worked so far, and Grady realized he needed to change his tactics. To this point, all that his anger and frustration had netted him was the silent treatment. He'd never known a woman who could say more without uttering a word.

Okay, okay, he was willing to admit he'd made mistakes, too. Earlier in the week Savannah had cooked him his favorite dinner as a peace offering, but he'd been so angry he'd chosen to overlook the gesture. He'd been wrong to ignore her outstretched hand, but he was man enough to admit it. He hoped to make peace with her now—hoped he could persuade her to see reason.

Savannah had given him the cold shoulder since he'd walked in on her and Smith in the kitchen. For the rest of the day she'd conveniently disappeared and had retired to her room as soon as it was dark. She wasn't asleep; he could hear her moving about upstairs, as restless as he was here below.

He continued pacing, then decided to talk to her now, before the opportunity was lost. Before he changed his mind. He headed up the stairs, taking them two at a time, paused outside her bedroom, inhaled deeply and knocked. Loudly.

"Yes?" his sister said through the door. Her voice was anything but warm, and the door stayed closed.

"Savannah, I'd appreciate the opportunity to discuss the matter of Laredo Smith with you," he said. It'd taken him ten minutes to come up with those words, to strike the proper tone. He thought he sounded formal, calm, even lawyerly.

The door opened and she stood stiffly in the doorway, blocking the entrance. "Downstairs might be more comfortable," he suggested, gesturing down the narrow staircase.

She hesitated, then reluctantly nodded.

Grady relaxed slightly, and wondered how much this peace was going to cost him. Being on the outs with his only sister distressed him more than he cared to reveal.

Savannah followed him down the stairs and took a seat on the sofa. "You owe me an apology, Grady."

"All right, all right," he said, raising both arms in surrender. "I apologize."

"How about apologizing to Laredo?"

That was going too far, but Grady was smart enough to see that arguing the point wouldn't serve his purpose. "I want to discuss Laredo," he said again, and because it was impossible to hold still, he stood up and resumed his pacing. This next part was the most difficult. "I'm worried about you," he said.

"I'm thirty-one years old and I don't need my brother treating me like a child. You're not my guardian. I was mortified today, Grady. Simply mortified."

His behavior had embarrassed him, too, but he hadn't been able to prevent it. Walking into the house and finding Savannah in a man's arms had been a shock.

"I apologize," he muttered again. He walked the full length of the room and turned back.

"Then why did you act like…like a bull on the rampage?"

Grady didn't know what to tell her other than the truth. "I'm afraid you're going to be hurt."

"My life is none of your concern."

On the contrary, he thought, what happened to her was very much his concern. He was her brother. She was naive about men—especially con artists like Laredo Smith—and whether she realized it or not, she needed him. At least he could be counted on to keep a level head. "Savannah, you're setting yourself up for heartache, getting involved with a drifter."

She sighed as if to say he clearly had no concept of how she felt. Perhaps he didn't, but that didn't change the facts.

"Laredo's been the perfect gentleman," she explained calmly. "I was crying and he comforted me."

"He made you cry?"

"No." The word was filled with exasperation. "I told him about Richard, and I always cry when I talk about Richard."

Grady's jaw tightened at the mention of his younger brother, but he didn't want to discuss him now. He crossed to Savannah and squatted down in front of her. "Savannah, look at me."

"I like Laredo."

"I know you do, and that's what troubles me."

"But why? Haven't you seen how hard he's worked in my garden? He's done nothing but show me kindness."

Grady ground his teeth in frustration. "There are things about him you don't know," he said as gently as he could.

"Grady, look at me, really look. My youth is slipping

through my fingers and I've been given this…this precious gift, this blessing, a chance to love and be loved. I'm not going to let you or anyone else ruin it for me."

"Love." The word felt like acid on his tongue. "You *love* him? You hardly know him!"

She lowered her gaze to her clenched hands. "I *could* love him, I know I could, and he could love me, too. He understands me and I understand him."

"You've known him what? Three days? Four? Savannah, for crying out loud, what's happened to you?"

She looked at him then, and to his amazement she smiled. "Something wonderful, Grady, something really wonderful." She touched his arm and nearly blinded him with the brilliance of her smile. "I feel alive, truly alive for the first time in years. I'd forgotten how good it felt."

"Savannah, Savannah," he moaned. She made this so damned difficult.

"Grady, please be happy for me."

"I can't."

"Then don't ruin it for me, please. That's all I ask."

He stood, feeling the pain of what he had to tell her until the words felt like bricks loaded on his back. "You can't trust him."

"How can you say that?" Her face wore a look of pure puzzlement. "Laredo's been nothing but trustworthy."

"You can't trust him," Grady repeated.

"I'd trust him with my life. Do you honestly think I'm such a bad judge of character? He's patient and generous, and for you to say otherwise proves you don't really know him."

"You're naive. He'll use you, and when he's finished, he'll leave you to face the consequences alone."

His words were followed by a shocked angry silence. Then she said, "That comment was unworthy of you."

Well, she'd wait a long time before he'd apologize. He hated what he had to tell her next. Hated to be the one to destroy the fairy tale she'd built around this cast-off cowboy. "Ask me where I was this afternoon," he demanded.

Savannah blinked. "Where were you?"

"I stopped off at Cal Patterson's to make a phone call."

"You couldn't do it here?"

"No. Cal's got the names and phone numbers of all the district members in the cattlemen's association." He waited until the information sank in.

"You tried to find out about Laredo," she said, and her voice dropped to a whisper.

"Savannah, listen to me. It gives me no joy to tell you this, but your precious Laredo Smith was fired from his last job."

She remained outwardly calm, but Grady noticed her clenched hands in her lap. "I talked to Earl Chesterton myself," he continued. "Smith was fired and for a damn good reason." If that didn't convince her of the truth about this man, nothing would.

A moment of shocked silence followed, or what he mistook for shock. To his amazement, Savannah slowly smiled. "Oh, Grady, how worried you must have been, but there was no need. I already knew all about that."

Chapter Four

Grady wasn't looking forward to talking to Frank Hennessey, but he'd delayed his visit to the sheriff long enough. His fingers tightened on the steering wheel as he drove toward town, and his thoughts darkened with his fears. It bothered him that his sensible, intelligent sister had been taken in by a lowlife like Smith.

One thing Grady couldn't tolerate was a thief. As far as he was concerned, stealing what belonged to another was about as low as a man could go. His feelings, no doubt, were influenced by what Richard had done. From the time his younger brother was an infant, he'd been spoiled and coddled by their parents. Savannah was guilty of catering to him, as well—along with everyone else. Even in high school, when Richard should have been maturing and accepting adult responsibilities, he'd made it an art form to pawn off his obligations on others. From early childhood Richard had charmed his way through life. How that boy could talk, Grady recalled cynically. He'd often watched in astonishment as Richard, so glib and smooth, managed to get out of one scrape after another. Nothing had been his fault. Someone else was always to blame. His brother had continually found ways to shift the responsibility for his failures and problems onto other people.

Richard was a charmer, a ladies' man and a smooth talker, but Grady had never suspected his brother was a thief. Then he'd learned the truth. After the shock of the theft had worn off, Grady had been left to face the reality of their dire financial circumstances. He'd even blamed himself. He should never have taken Richard to the Brewster bank or let him know where he kept the key to the safe-deposit box. But Grady had trusted him. And learned the hard way that it had been a mistake.

He wasn't willing to make a second mistake, especially not where his sister was concerned. Savannah was all the family he had left, and he wasn't going to lose her.

In the beginning Grady's opinion of this outsider had been tainted by Savannah's attitude. For the first time in more years than he could remember, she'd challenged his judgment. So Grady's natural inclination was to dislike the man she'd favored, against his advice. But he *had* tolerated Laredo Smith's presence. He'd even taken some good-natured ribbing from Wiley and Caroline Daniels about being unreasonable. Given time, he might have put the drifter on the payroll himself. As Wiley and Savannah had reminded him often enough, they needed extra help.

He wouldn't hire Smith now, though. Not after what he'd learned. No way in hell would he offer a job to a known thief.

Grady had discovered everything he needed to know about Laredo Smith in his short conversation with Earl Chesterton. He wanted Smith off his land as soon as possible and as far away from Savannah as could be arranged. Frank would understand, and because the sheriff was fond of Savannah, he'd be eager to help Grady send him packing.

His sister's words—*Don't ruin this for me*—echoed in Grady's head, and although he believed he was making the right choice, he felt a sense of guilt. The last thing he wanted was to see Savannah hurt. He wanted to get rid of this drifter, but he had to manage it in such a way that Savannah would agree it was the only prudent course of action.

For that he needed Frank Hennessey's help.

Grady considered it his duty to protect his sister. She claimed she knew everything necessary about Laredo; Grady doubted that. A thief was a thief, and if Smith had stolen once, he'd steal again. Grady strongly suspected this cowboy had tangled with the authorities on more than one occasion. That was what he intended to find out from Frank Hennessey. Faced with the raw truth, Savannah would have no qualms about sending Smith on his way.

Grady found Frank Hennessey relaxing at his oak desk, feet propped on the edge and hat lowered over his eyes as he enjoyed a midafternoon snooze. Frank had represented the law in Promise for as long as Grady could remember, and while an able lawman, he took business in his stride.

Grady closed the door a little harder than necessary and Frank used his index finger to lift his Stetson off his forehead just enough to let him take a peek at his visitor.

"Howdy." Frank greeted him lazily with the familiarity that years of friendship allowed. "What can I do for you, Grady?"

Grady hesitated, unsure how to begin. At last he blurted, "I've got trouble."

The older man's smile faded and he slowly straightened. "What kind of trouble?"

Grady removed his hat and rubbed a hand across his

brow. "I need to ask a favor of you, Frank. Now, I know you wouldn't normally do this sort of thing, but it's the only way I can think of to save Savannah."

"What's wrong with Savannah?" Frank asked abruptly, gesturing toward the hard wooden chair that sat alongside his desk.

It gave Grady no pleasure to drag family business into the open; however, he had no choice but to involve Frank. "You've heard about Savannah hiring a drifter to work in her rose garden?"

Frank's mouth angled into a half smile. "The story's been all around town twice by now, and Dovie was full of the news." He paused to chuckle appreciatively. "Apparently Dovie didn't think Savannah had it in her to stand up to you."

Grady hated the thought of folks talking about Savannah behind her back and let Frank know his feelings on the matter with a dark scowl.

Apparently Frank got the message because he cleared his throat and looked apologetic. "You know how women love to gossip," he said with a disapproving frown—although it was well-known that the sheriff wasn't opposed to indulging in the habit himself.

The fact that the news had spread all over town complicated things. Grady figured all he could do now was get to the point and leave the problem in Frank's capable hands.

"I don't trust him. First off, I've got to think Smith's a phony name."

"He might have picked something more original than Smith if that's the case, don't you think?" Frank asked, rubbing his chin thoughtfully.

"Why he chose that name isn't the point," Grady argued. "'Laredo Smith' sounds about as real as a three-dollar bill."

"Other than not liking his name, have you got a reason not to trust him?" Frank asked next.

"Plenty." Surely Frank didn't think he'd come to him over something trivial! "Smith mentioned that he last worked for Earl Chesterton on the Triple C over in Williamsburg, so I called Earl and talked to him myself. Found out Earl fired Laredo Smith for stealing." He spit out the last word. Even saying it left a bad taste in his mouth.

Frank's eyebrows lifted. "Why didn't Earl press charges?"

"I asked him that myself." The other rancher would have saved Grady a great deal of trouble if he had. "Apparently it was one man's word against another's and no way to prove who was telling the truth and who wasn't. Earl fired them both."

"I see," Frank murmured. "Seems to me that if Smith had something to hide, he wouldn't have mentioned working on the Triple C."

Grady sighed and wondered why no one else viewed the situation with the same concern he did. "I'm asking you to do a background check on Smith," he said, and realized he was expecting a great deal of their friendship. Frank had every right to deny his request, but Grady hoped he wouldn't.

The sheriff frowned and his chair creaked noisily as he leaned back and considered Grady's request. "I understand you're worried about Savannah and I can't say I blame you. Your sister is one of the most kindhearted people I know, and if this saddle bum hurts her, he'll have me and half the town to deal with."

"You'll do it, then?" Grady said with relief.

"I'll check him out," Frank said reluctantly.

The two exchanged handshakes and Grady left. On his way out of town, he decided to stop off at the post office and talk to Caroline. If he couldn't get through to his sister, maybe her best friend could. Reversing direction, he headed down Maple, then sat in the parking lot, debating the wisdom of his decision. In the past year or so he'd begun to notice Caroline Daniels. She was younger than Savannah, and while they'd been friends for several years, he'd always thought of her as a kid. For some time now it'd become difficult to view Caroline as anything but an attractive woman.

However, Caroline was also opinionated and headstrong. More often than not, her views clashed with his own, and as a result, they argued frequently. Another problem existed, as well.

Maggie.

Grady enjoyed the five-year-old, but for reasons he didn't understand, the little girl was terrified of him. Savannah baby-sat her on Monday nights while Caroline did volunteer work, and it had reached the point that Grady stayed out of sight rather than intimidate the little girl.

Things being what they were, it was a risk to ask for Caroline's help, but one he was willing to take. More than anything, asking Caroline to join forces with him proved how desperate he'd grown to get Savannah to see reason.

Thankfully Caroline was alone when he approached the front counter.

"Hello, Grady," she said, glancing up from the mail she was sorting.

"Have you had lunch yet?" he asked.

Her eyes widened—but she was no more surprised by his invitation than he was himself.

"It's three-thirty."

"Coffee, then," he suggested gruffly, feeling gauche for not looking at the time. No wonder his stomach growled; he'd missed lunch entirely. Which also went to show how desperate he'd become.

"I don't suppose it'd hurt if I took a few minutes off," she said, and set the mail aside.

Definitely curious, Caroline invited him behind the counter. She located a clean mug for him in the back room and filled his cup and her own. "What's on your mind?" she asked.

"Savannah." Grady couldn't see any need to beat around the bush. "I'm worried about her and that drifter."

"He has a name," Caroline said, stirring a spoonful of sugar into her coffee.

"Sure. *Smith.*"

"Laredo Smith."

"All right, Laredo Smith," he said impatiently. Grady didn't know what it was about Caroline that attracted and irritated him at the same time. Lately he found it difficult to carry on a decent conversation with the woman, although he did actually like her.

"What's the problem?" Caroline asked, her eyes meeting his above the rim of her mug.

"I'm afraid he's going to abuse her generosity." In Grady's opinion, the wrangler was already guilty of that and more.

"Don't you trust your sister's judgment?"

"Of course," he flared. "It's just that she's naive and vulnerable. Savannah doesn't have a lot of experience with men, especially smooth talkers like Laredo Smith."

"Laredo's a smooth talker?" Caroline echoed. "I hadn't noticed." The mug was at her lips again, and it seemed to him she purposely held it there to hide a smile. Apparently his concern for Savannah amused her.

"Is something funny?" he challenged, disliking the way she made him the target of her humor.

"Of course not." The amusement left her eyes, replaced by a mock seriousness that infuriated him even more.

"I can see coming here was a mistake," he said, putting the mug down with a clatter. "I should have known you'd find this all a joke." He turned away, but she stopped him.

"Grady."

He hesitated.

"Listen, I doubt there's as much to worry about as you think. Savannah's the most levelheaded person I know."

Grady used to believe the same thing. "She's not herself. He's changed her."

"Yes, he has," Caroline admitted.

At last they could agree on something. "Then you know what I'm saying?"

"Grady," she said, her look gentle, "Laredo *has* changed Savannah, but he's changed her for the better. Don't you see how happy she is? You can't be around her and not feel it. I might not be the best judge of character, but I don't think Laredo is evil incarnate the way you seem to. Maggie was full of stories about him Monday night after I picked her up. She thought he was great. It isn't every man who'd sit and read to a five-year-old until she fell asleep. Savannah said the three of them spent an hour in the calving barn, showing Maggie the newborn calves."

"In other words she likes Smith," Grady muttered.

Maggie liked Smith but not him. Caroline apparently didn't realize the insult she'd delivered.

"It's much more than that."

"Really?" He didn't even try to hide his sarcasm.

"What is it you're really afraid of?" she asked.

For the first time Caroline sounded concerned. He held her gaze a long time, then finally said, "I don't want anyone to take advantage of her."

"She's old enough to know her own mind."

"She's too damn trusting."

"Is that bad?"

"Yes," he stormed. "I'm afraid he's going to take advantage of her. I'm afraid Savannah's going to end up alone and pregnant."

The eyes that had just a moment ago revealed the first shred of understanding and compassion flickered with a jolt of unanticipated pain. It took Grady only an instant to realize what he'd said.

"In other words you're afraid your sister will end up like me?"

Grady struggled for the words to apologize. They didn't come easy to a man like him. "I didn't mean that the way it sounded," he said.

"Of course you did."

He probably should have left well enough alone, but he was desperate and he knew Savannah would listen to Caroline before she would him. "Will you talk to her?" he asked hopefully. At her absent look he continued, "About getting rid of Smith before he can hurt her."

"No," she said flat out.

"No?"

"You heard me. If I was going to talk to anyone about this, it'd be you." Caroline's voice gained strength.

"And what I'd say, Grady, is leave Savannah to live her own life."

"And make a fool of herself?"

"Yes, if that's what it takes. She's not a child to be chastised and ridiculed; she's a woman with a woman's heart. Grady, I swear if you do anything to spoil her chance of finding happiness, I'll never forgive you."

"Happiness with a saddle bum like Smith?" He might have laughed if there'd been any humor in the suggestion.

"Yes," Caroline responded without hesitation.

Furious, more with himself than with Caroline, Grady stalked out of the office. He should have known better than try to reason with Savannah's best friend. She was as stubborn as his sister. And less tactful about it, too.

"GOOD AFTERNOON, Laredo," Savannah said shyly as she joined him in her rose garden. She carried out a tray and two tall glasses of iced tea. Rocket was at her side, so old now that he found it difficult to move. Generally he stayed in the house, but he appeared to be a little more energetic than usual just now and had followed her outside and into the warm sunshine.

Laredo's efforts were in evidence in every corner of her small paradise. Never had her garden looked more beautiful. The beds were meticulously groomed. Even the roses themselves had responded to his care. They'd burst into flower days earlier than anticipated. Some would claim it was due to the unusually warm spring, but Savannah chose to believe it was because of the love and care she and Laredo had given them.

"Afternoon," he said, leaning on the hoe.

It never failed. Her heart—like her beautiful roses—bloomed with excitement and joy whenever she saw him. He was tall and strong and lovely. She realized that "lovely" wasn't a word often associated with men, but she could find none more appropriate. Beyond everything else Laredo had given her, the most precious was the way she felt around him. Savannah had never considered herself beautiful, but that was how he made her feel. Beautiful. Feminine. Desirable.

"Would you like some iced tea?" she asked.

"That'd be great." He set the hoe aside, removed the tray from her hands and led the way to the small wrought-iron table in the farthest corner of the garden. She'd purposely placed it there amidst the old roses in order to enjoy their fragrance and special beauty. Rocket followed them there and with a groan sank down in the table's shade.

"I'm about finished with the hoeing," Laredo said, bending down to stroke the dog's ears.

This was a problem. He completed each task with speed, skill and determination. She longed to urge him to slow down, to linger over each small assignment so that the work would last, but he never did. From the first he'd set out to prove his worth and he'd done so, many times over.

Another day, two at the most, and he'd have completed her list. Everything thereafter would be a make-work project. Not that she couldn't come up with some.

"Wiley stopped by earlier," he said, and downed half the tea in a series of deep swallows. He wiped the back of his hand across his mouth, then leaned forward and stroked Rocket's ears again. Savannah's gaze rested on the dog who'd once belonged to her father and she smiled as he snored softly, already asleep.

"He told me about Roanie's sore leg and he asked me to look at it. You don't mind, do you?"

If anything, Savannah was relieved. All three realized

it'd be best if Grady didn't know about Laredo doctoring one of the horses. Nevertheless it'd be a shame to let the old roan suffer. Especially when Laredo could help— save them the expense of calling the vet.

"Of course I don't mind," she assured him.

"I'll probably need to rub in some ointment and wrap up the leg."

She nodded. "I'm grateful." If Grady wouldn't say it, she would, but her appreciation extended far beyond any expertise Laredo offered in the area of horses. He'd blessed her life in the week since his arrival. One week. Seven fleeting days, and yet it felt as though he'd always been part of her life. People would say it was fanciful or ridiculous, but in an odd way, Savannah felt as if her life had been on hold while she waited for Laredo to find her.

She smiled to herself, amused that Grady was making such a fool of himself, all the while calling *her* the fool. Considering the fuss her older brother had made, anyone would think she'd become Laredo's lover when in reality he hadn't so much as kissed her.

But she wished he would…. She'd dreamed of it endlessly, hungering for his touch. Grady had chastised her for claiming to love Laredo on such short acquaintance, and for the first time in recent memory she'd lied to her brother. She'd told him she didn't love Laredo but that she could.

The truth was she *did* love him. She loved him for the gentle care he gave her roses. For his loving way with animals. For his honesty. For his tender patience with Maggie and, most important, for the joy he'd brought into her life. Each day she awoke happy and excited, knowing he'd be in the kitchen to greet her. Each night she laid her head on her pillow, her mind full of dreams she'd never dared to believe possible, never believed were meant for a woman like her.

So, while it was true he hadn't touched her except for that one time he'd held her in the kitchen, she knew instinctively that he shared her feelings. She felt his love in a thousand ways. Unspoken, but real. As intense as her own for him.

Yes, Grady had called her a fool, and perhaps she was. But if being considered a fool meant she was this happy, then he could call her whatever name he liked.

"Is there anything more I can do for you this afternoon?" Laredo asked.

She shook her head. "I'll be leaving soon."

"If you're going into town, would you mind checking on my truck at Powell's Garage?"

"I...I can do that for you later in the week, if you want, but I wasn't planning on going into town." Savannah had hoped to avoid any questions about her destination. She'd hoped to slip quietly away and return to the ghost town. It had taken her a full week to gather the courage to go back, but despite her reservations, she'd decided to do it. She was sure there were more old roses to be found.

"Savannah," Laredo said, touching her hand. "You're headed back to Bitter End, aren't you?"

She lowered her eyes and nodded, knowing that, like Grady, he'd disapprove. "I want to look for more roses. If the plants in the cemetery survived, there're bound to be others." In the days since her last visit Savannah had managed to convince herself that the darkness, the sense of oppression, had come from her own imagination. It'd been nerves and excitement, that was all. Grady had warned her about the ghost town so often that her head had been filled with nonsense. After a while she'd come to believe it. And even if what she'd experienced was real, she'd managed the first time and would again.

"Your brother—"

"Grady disapproves of a great deal in my life just now. I'm going back to Bitter End, Laredo, with or without Grady's approval."

The strength of her objection appeared to catch him unawares. "Surely your brother has a reason for not wanting you there?"

"You know Grady," she answered. "He's overprotective."

"I don't know your brother," Laredo told her quietly, "but everything he says and does is because he loves you and is concerned about you. It might be best to heed his advice."

If Savannah hadn't fallen in love with Laredo already, she would have lost her heart right then and there. He'd defended Grady, when Grady had done nothing but cause him problems.

"He doesn't understand," she murmured.

"Where is this place?" Laredo asked. "I haven't heard anyone else talk about a ghost town in this area."

"I don't think many people know about it." Grady had located the town as a teenager and promised he'd take her there himself. It was the only time she could remember her brother breaking his word. "Grady was there once, but he refused to talk about it afterward. No matter how much I pleaded, he refused to give in. All he'd say was that he was never going back and he certainly wasn't going to take his little sister there."

"Then how'd you find the place?"

She laughed lightly. "It wasn't easy. It took me weeks."

"Why now? Because of the old roses?"

Savannah smiled. "I read an article in one of my gardening magazines about a man who found a huge number of old roses in a ghost-town cemetery. I'd nearly forgotten about Bitter End, but once I remembered, I couldn't stop thinking about it. I asked Grady as much as I could without arousing his suspicions, but eventually he caught on and wouldn't give me any more information."

Laredo frowned. "Savannah," he pleaded, "if your brother's that worried about it, then so am I. Don't go."

Her heart sank. Not Laredo, too. "Please don't ask that of me," she whispered.

He got up and walked around the table to stand in front of her. "Then don't do it alone," he said urgently.

"But there isn't anyone—"

"There's me."

Savannah leaned back to see him more clearly. "You'd do that for me?"

He nodded and knelt in front of her, his expression earnest. "Promise me, Savannah."

"I promise." She needed to touch him. She couldn't have explained why, but the yearning inside her was too strong to ignore. Hesitantly she pressed one hand to his cheek, her palm curving around his jaw. The skin was stubbled with his beard, and yet she'd never felt anything more sensual.

Laredo closed his eyes and gripped her wrist with a strength she hadn't expected. "You make it damn near impossible," he said from between clenched teeth.

"Impossible?" she whispered. She found it difficult to breathe or swallow. Her heart beat at an alarming rate, and she feared he would guess how his closeness unnerved her.

"Don't you know?" His words were half groan, half speech, as if her touching him, even in the most innocent way, caused him pain. She felt the urgency in him and the restraint. She honored him for that restraint—but she didn't need it anymore.

"I want you to kiss me, Laredo. I've dreamed about you every night." Her raspy voice was barely audible.

"Savannah, please."

"Please what? Ignore my heart? I can't! I tried, Laredo, I really did."

He cradled her face, and their eyes met. In his she read determination and a kind of desperation. "Grady's made it difficult enough for you," he said. "I can't, I won't make it—"

"I don't care what my brother thinks," she choked out, stopping him by placing her fingertips to his lips. "I know my heart, Laredo, and my heart wants you very much."

His hands slid from the sides of her face and into her hair. Then slowly, inch by thrilling inch, he brought her mouth to his.

The instant their lips touched, Savannah felt her heart leap with a burst of joy. It overtook her, drove everything else from her mind.

His mouth was warm and moist, and he tasted of iced tea and fresh mint. He moved his lips hungrily against hers, molding her mouth to his with a heat that seared her senses. Although her experience with lovemaking had been limited, she'd had her share of kisses. But never like this. Never with this kind of heat, this degree of passion. Had it happened with anyone else, it would have frightened her.

Soon their arms were wrapped completely around each other in a struggle to get closer. She realized the fierceness with which they clung must be hurting his ribs. She tried to say something, to shift her hands, but he wouldn't allow it, his movements urging her to hold him closer, hold him tighter.

The kiss grew hotter and hotter as they each sought to give more, take more, be more. Laredo's breath came hard and fast. Her own echoed his.

With a moan, Laredo finally broke away, his shoulders heaving. "That shouldn't have happened," he said in a tortured voice. "I don't want to hurt you."

"You could never hurt me," she assured him, her face against his chest. In all her days she'd never been more brazen with a man, asking him outright to kiss her, to hold her. But hard as she tried, Savannah couldn't make herself regret what she'd done. If anything she wondered why it had taken her so long. She'd had no idea kissing could be this...incredible. Her friends should have told her!

"Say something," she pleaded. "I need to know you're feeling it, too."

"I think I knew the minute you stopped to offer me a ride." He got to his feet and walked away from her.

"Laredo?"

"I promised Wiley I'd check on Roanie. Remember?"

In other words their discussion was over; he had nothing more to say. Nor did he wish to hear what *she* might say. "All right," she said, hanging her head in defeat.

He got as far as the garden gate, then turned back. "You won't go to the ghost town without me?"

"No," she promised.

He nodded. He seemed about to speak again but hesitated. If he dared apologize for kissing her, she didn't know what she'd do. Probably scream in frustration. That would be an unprecedented event—Savannah Weston screaming! She gave an involuntary giggle.

Savannah watched him leave, then carried the tray of

empty glasses back into the house. Despite his withdrawal, his abrupt departure, she felt like dancing around her kitchen. He'd kissed her! And it had been wonderful.

Not only had Laredo kissed her, he'd said he'd been thinking about it for days. The same as she had. That was enough to make her heart wild with joy. But there was more. He'd as much as said he loved her.

"Oh, please," she prayed, closing her eyes and clasping her hands, "let it be true. Don't let this be a cruel joke." But she knew otherwise; she'd felt it in the wonder of his kiss.

With the afternoon free, Savannah baked chocolate-chip cookies, one of her many specialties. She tucked a dozen inside the freezer to save for Maggie's visits and filled the cookie jar with the rest.

Because the kitchen door was open, she heard Grady's truck pull into the yard, followed by his near-frantic shout.

"Savannah!"

It wasn't her name that shook her, but the way he yelled it. Rushing to the door, she found him stalking toward the house.

"Grady, for heaven's sake, what's wrong?"

"You're not to talk to him!"

"Grady," she said, her patience gone. "We've already had this discussion. Laredo—"

"Not *Laredo*," he barked as if she were slow-witted or being purposely obtuse.

"*Who?*"

"Richard."

"Richard?" She saw him then, her younger brother. Her "big boy," the baby she'd loved and cared for and spoiled. He walked slowly down the long driveway, hefting his suitcase, eyes focused on the house as if the sight of it was the only thing that kept him on his feet.

"Richard," she cried, and pressed her hands to her mouth. "Grady, how could you drive past him like that?"

"He's not welcome here, Savannah."

"Grady, he's our *brother.*" Not caring what he thought, she flew out the door and raced down the stairs. Richard. He was here at last. Now they'd learn the truth, the real truth, and everything would be right with their world again.

Richard had come home.

Chapter Five

Richard had changed, Savannah mused. Although dusty from the road and weary to the bone, he'd acquired a look of sophistication she hadn't seen six years ago. This was Richard, her brother, but at the same time he was someone she no longer knew. None of that mattered, however, the instant he wrapped his arms around her and joyously hugged her close. Her tears mingled with laughter and pleas that he put her down.

"Savannah, oh, it's so good to see you." His face brightened with excitement. "You're even more beautiful than I remembered."

Wiping the tears from her cheek, she smiled up at him. "I can't believe it's you."

"I'm home. You have no idea how good this old place looks." He gazed longingly toward the house.

Her heart warmed in that moment, and she was almost willing to forgive him the agony his betrayal had cost them.

"Don't get comfortable, little brother." Grady's eyes were savage. He stood on the top step, feet apart, arms akimbo, barring the door.

Slowly Richard set Savannah away from him and faced his brother.

"Grady," she said in warning. Despite his faults, Richard *was* their brother and the least they could do was hear him out. "Give him a chance to explain."

Richard looked from brother to sister. He advanced slowly toward Grady, then paused. "I don't blame you, Grady. You have every right to be angry."

"You've got that straight."

"What I did was despicable." Richard stretched out his arm to Savannah, as if he needed her to stand with him. She stepped to his side, wanting to right the past and thrust all the ugliness behind them. They were a family, and if they couldn't forgive one another, then they'd be hypocrites to sit in church every Sunday. The Good Book was full of the power of forgiveness. Only this wasn't what Grady wanted to hear. Not now. Not yet. He demanded his pound of flesh first, and while Savannah understood his anger, she wanted him to give Richard the opportunity to set things straight.

"Despicable is only one in a long list of words that come to mind when I think of you." Grady's face was hard and unyielding. He'd braced his feet apart in a way that said it would take the strength of ten men to budge him from that porch. Nothing Richard could say would change his mind. Savannah had bumped against that pride of his often enough to know. Unless something drastic happened, Grady wouldn't let Richard set foot in the home where he was born and raised.

Her younger brother hung his head in shame. "I don't blame you for hating me."

"Oh, Richard, you don't know how difficult it was for us," Savannah said, despite her determination to hold her tongue.

Richard's face crumpled with regret. "I'm so sorry. I was young and stupid, and then once I owned up to what

I'd done...I couldn't face you and Grady. I was too ashamed.''

"You stole that money from your own flesh and blood!" Grady spit out.

"I was crazy with grief," Richard pleaded, sounding the same way he had as a child when he knew he'd done something wrong. "I didn't think. All I knew was that Mom and Dad were gone."

"And Dad had stored away a hunk of cash," Grady said.

Richard gestured weakly. "I was never cut out to be a cowboy, even you have to admit that," he said, and glanced up at Grady for confirmation. "I could read the writing on the wall. With Dad gone you'd expect me to help around the place, and it just wasn't in me. Still isn't. Cows and me never saw eye to eye. You said it more than once yourself." He gave a crooked half smile, enticing Grady to agree with him.

Grady remained cold and silent, his eyes as hard as flint.

"I know it was wrong to take that money. A thousand times since, I've cursed myself for being so stupid, so greedy."

"You should have phoned," Savannah chastised. "You could have let us know where you were. Grady and I were worried sick." She looked to her brother to continue, to explain what they'd endured because of Richard.

Once again Grady's cool silence was answer enough.

"I thought about coming home," Richard said in a small pleading voice. "You don't know how many times I've thought of it. You're right, Savannah," he said, rushing his words. "I should've called. I know that now, but

I was afraid of what you'd say. I didn't have the courage to face you."

"What happened to the money?" Grady threw the question at his brother with a vengeance.

"The money," Richard repeated, and the sigh that followed said it all.

"You blew it," Grady said with disgust.

"I put it up as capital in a business venture. My plan," he said, glancing desperately to Savannah and then Grady, "was to triple it and share the profits with you two. I thought if I did that, you'd forgive me and let me come home. Then we could go on the way we always have. But—" he paused and looked away "—the venture went sour."

"In other words you lost everything."

Richard nodded slowly. "The investment wasn't as solid as I was led to believe. It was a bitter lesson. But you have to understand," he added, motioning toward Grady, "I was desperate to come home." His voice shook as though the memory was as painful to him as it was to Savannah and Grady. "By this time I missed you both so much I would have done anything to find a way home."

"You could have written," Savannah said. "Even if you weren't ready to talk to us..." For months she'd prayed for a letter, a phone call, anything that would explain what had happened. She'd refused to give up hope, refused to believe Richard would steal from them and then just disappear. After six months she stopped making excuses, and when they hadn't heard from him after a year, his name was dropped from their conversations.

"I *wanted* to write," Richard said, leaping on her words. "I tried. As God is my witness, I tried, but I was never good with words. How could I possibly explain everything in a letter?''

Grady snickered loudly. "Seems to me you're about as slick with words as a snake-oil salesman."

A flash of pain appeared in Richard's eyes. "You really hate me, don't you, Grady?"

"How could we hate you?" Savannah answered in Grady's stead, fearing his response. "You're our brother."

At her words Richard rallied somewhat and gazed around the yard. "You've obviously done all right by yourselves. The ranch looks great."

"No thanks to you."

"Think about it, Grady," Richard challenged. "What good would I have been to you if I'd stuck around? As far as I'm concerned, cows smell bad, have a negative disposition and are always needing something done to them. If I'd stayed, I wouldn't have been any help. Okay, I admit taking the money was pretty underhand, but all I really did was lay claim to part of my inheritance a little early."

"We almost lost the ranch," Savannah felt obliged to tell him. Surely he must have realized that? "Richard, I don't think you have a clue how hard it's been for Grady and me," she said.

"I'm sorry," he repeated with what sounded like genuine regret. "How many times do I need to say it?"

"Sorry?" Grady said the word as though it were the foulest obscenity.

Richard ignored the outburst. "I'll admit that what I did was rotten, but would it really have been such a bad thing if you'd been forced to sell the land?"

"What do you *mean?*" Savannah asked, certain she wasn't hearing him correctly. This land had been in the

Weston family for generations. Their ancestors had settled here, worked the land, raised cattle. Generations of Westons had been buried here in a small cemetery plot overlooking the main pasture. This land was their heritage, their birthright. Their future. That Richard could suggest selling it revealed how little he understood or appreciated the legacy.

"These days everyone knows its not a good idea to eat a lot of red meat," he explained when it became apparent that his words had upset her. "The beef industry's been declining steadily for some time, or so I hear. Actually I'm surprised you've held on to the old place this long."

Savannah's heart sank. It seemed impossible that Richard shared the same blood that flowed through Grady's veins and hers. But he was her brother and she refused to turn her back on him, despite his shortcomings. Despite his betrayal.

"You think because you say you're sorry it makes everything right?" Grady asked, his voice shaking with such rage Savannah feared he was near exploding. "Do you honestly believe you can walk back into our lives as if you'd done nothing wrong? I'm here to tell you it's not going to happen."

Confused and uncertain, Richard looked to his sister for support. "But I'm willing to do whatever's necessary to make it up to you."

"Give me back six years of constant hard work," Grady shouted. "Days that stretched fifteen hours without rest. Days in which I did the work of two men. Backbreaking work. Can you do *that*, little brother?"

Richard stood still and silent.

"For six long years I fought off the wolf at the door. For six years I dealt with grief and stress and worry so bad I couldn't sleep." He climbed down the steps, one step for each statement. Anger seethed below the surface unlike anything she'd ever seen in Grady. Not the explosive kind common with him, but the deep bitter anger that gnawed at a man's soul.

"I can't change the past," Richard muttered, his shoulders hunched, "but I'd hoped we could put all this behind us and start fresh."

"Not on your life," Grady said. He stood face-to-face with Richard now, glaring at him. "You haven't shown any true regret. Not once have you asked Savannah and me to forgive you. As far as I'm concerned, you got your inheritance, and you wasted it. Now get off *our* land."

"You want me to leave?" Richard sounded incredulous. He looked at Savannah but she turned away. "You're my family!" he cried. "The only family I've got. You don't mean this. Okay, okay, you're right, I should have asked you to forgive me. I meant to—that was the real reason I returned. Like I said, I want to make it up to both of you."

Savannah wavered, ambivalent.

"You should have thought of that sooner," Grady replied, his voice clipped.

She'd hoped they could resolve their differences and make Richard a part of their lives again, but Grady was right. Richard hadn't revealed any sincere sorrow for the agony he'd caused them. But then he'd always been weak and easily influenced. Nevertheless he was their brother; it came down to that. If for no other reason than to honor the memory of their parents, she wanted there to be no ill will between them.

"You're serious?" Richard's face clouded with disbelief. "You want me off the ranch?"

"I've never been more serious in my life."

Brother stared down brother.

"I...I'm without a job. I was working at...at a sales job, and they downsized. I don't have anywhere to go. I left instructions for the check from my severance package to be mailed here." He glanced hopefully at Savannah and then at Grady.

Savannah silently pleaded with Grady, but he refused to look in her direction. It was hell staying quiet, especially when Richard begged for her help.

"You, too, Savannah?" he whispered in the hurt voice that tugged at her heart. "Do you want me to leave, too?"

Savannah was in torment, not knowing how to respond. Of course she wanted him to stay, wanted their lives to return to the way they'd been before. But she didn't know if that was possible.

"I'm ruined," he whispered brokenly. "The money's gone. I lost my job and I have no savings. All I could think about was getting back to you and Grady. Making things right again."

Tears filled her eyes and she bit her lip, trapped as she was between the strong wills of her two brothers.

Not waiting for her reply, Richard leaned down and reached for his suitcase. Apparently he was weaker than they realized because he staggered, but caught himself in time to keep from collapsing.

Savannah could hold her tongue no longer. "Grady, please! He's about to faint. One night," she begged, sliding her arm around Richard's waist. "Let him stay one night."

For a moment she didn't think Grady would relent. "All right," he gave in, his reluctance clear, "but he sleeps in the bunkhouse. First thing in the morning he's out of here. Understand?"

"Thank you, brother," Richard said softly. "You won't be sorry, I promise you that. I'll find a way to make it up to you and Savannah. I didn't know, didn't realize...I'll do whatever you want if you'll just let me stay. You're the only family I've got."

LAREDO HADN'T MEANT to listen in on the scene outside the house. But he'd been in the garden at the time, and it had been impossible to ignore. He wasn't sure what had finally occurred between Savannah and her two brothers, but the three had apparently come to some kind of understanding. He didn't see Savannah again until dinnertime, and when he entered the house, she was all aflutter. He smelled biscuits baking, their aroma more enticing to him than the world's most expensive perfume. An apple pie cooled on the kitchen counter beside a standing rib roast, recently taken from the oven.

When she saw him, her beautiful face brightened with a shy smile of welcome. "Richard's here."

"So I understand." Laredo had tried to put the events of the early afternoon behind him and hoped she had, as well. Kissing her had been a mistake, one he regretted. His weakness for her complicated an already difficult situation.

The last thing he wanted was to let her believe in something that could never be. His property—three hundred acres in Oklahoma—was waiting for him. That and his horse. They were all he had. And they were almost nothing compared to the Westons' huge spread. Compared to what Savannah had now. It would be cruel to mislead her into thinking she could be part of his future. But if the kissing continued, it'd be as hard for him to walk away as it would be for her to let him go.

"He hasn't eaten in two days," she said, explaining

the frenzy of cooking that had taken place that afternoon. "I baked his favorites just the way Mom would have."

"How's Grady dealing with this?"

A sadness came over her and some of the excitement drained from her voice. "Not very well, unfortunately. He won't let Richard stay more than the night. He's forcing him to sleep in the bunkhouse. Richard said he was willing to work for his keep, and I think if I reason with him, Grady might let him stay on until his severance check arrives. I'm hoping he will, but it's hard to tell with Grady."

"Savannah!" Footsteps echoed as Richard Weston bounded down the stairs from the upstairs bedroom and burst into the kitchen. "I found my old guitar." He slid the strap over his shoulder and ran the pick over the tight strings, laughing with childish delight.

"I couldn't make myself throw away your things," Savannah admitted.

Walking about in his stocking feet, Richard circled the kitchen playing a mellow country hit Laredo recognized from the early nineties. A song of Reba's, if memory served him.

The family resemblance was strong, Laredo noticed. Richard was a younger, slimmer, blonder version of Grady, good-looking and suave. Apparently he'd inherited a double portion of charm, as well. He serenaded his sister, causing Savannah to blush unmercifully. Laredo knew he should leave, but he found himself enjoying the scene.

When Richard finished the song, he set the guitar aside and glanced in Laredo's direction, his eyes questioning.

Savannah's gaze followed her brother's. "This is Laredo Smith," she said. She reached for Laredo's hand, tucking it in both of hers. "He works for me."

"Really, Savannah," Richard joked. "I never suspected my older sister would have her own boy-toy." He laughed then, as if he found the comment hilarious.

Any goodwill Laredo had felt toward the other man vanished with the ugly suggestiveness of his remark. Savannah's face turned a deep shade of scarlet, and it was all Laredo could do to keep his mouth shut.

"It's n-not that way with us," she stammered.

"Whatever you say, big sister," Richard responded. "Hey, when's dinner? I could eat the entire roast myself." He gripped Savannah by the shoulder and noisily kissed her cheek. "I can't tell you how good it is to be home. I've missed you, Savannah, almost as much as I've missed your melt-in-the-mouth buttermilk biscuits."

"I need to be getting back," Laredo said, eager to check on Roanie. "I just stopped by to tell you I won't be here for dinner."

"You won't?" Savannah's eyes pleaded with him, and he realized she'd been counting on his support at the dinner table. She appeared to have forgotten that Grady had no particular fondness for him, either. He wished he could help her, but feared he'd do her cause more harm than good.

"Wiley invited me to play poker with him and his friends tonight," he explained to justify his absence. "The game's over at the Double Z bunkhouse."

She forgave him with a brave smile. "Have fun."

"Will everything be all right here?" He watched Richard walk past Rocket and give the old dog a vicious shove with his foot. His anger flared again, but he said nothing.

"Everything's going to be just fine," Richard answered on her behalf. "Grady can be downright stubborn at times, but he'll come around. Don't worry, I'll make sure big brother doesn't hassle her.'' He placed his arm around his sister's shoulders and squeezed hard. Savannah winced and Laredo battled the urge to grab the man by the shirtfront and jerk him away.

ALTHOUGH LAREDO didn't see Savannah again that evening, it didn't mean she wasn't on his mind. He worried about her dinner with her brothers, which burdened his concentration to the point that he lost at poker. Twenty bucks was more than he could afford to throw away in a poker game. By the end of the evening he regretted accepting Wiley's invitation.

He and Wiley returned to find Richard in the bunkhouse, sitting on the edge of his bed, strumming his guitar and singing drunkenly at the top of his lungs. Wiley snorted in contempt and headed immediately for his small room. Richard didn't seem to notice. He interrupted his song every so often to reach for a whiskey bottle and gulp down a swig. He held it up in silent invitation when he saw Laredo.

"Care to join me?'' he asked. "I broke into Grady's private stock. By the time he misses it, we'll both be long gone.'' He laughed as if stealing liquor from his brother was some kind of triumph.

"No, thanks,'' Laredo muttered in disgust.

"I should've been a country singer,'' Richard announced at the end of a barely recognizable Garth Brooks tune. Not that his singing voice was all that unpleasant, but the words were badly slurred.

"I've got talent, you know?'' He lifted the bottle to his mouth, gulped down another swallow and threw back his head. "Ahh.'' He gave an exaggerated shudder. "Powerful stuff. My big brother only buys the best.'' He set the guitar down on the floor, holding it carelessly by the neck.

Laredo was tired; he'd put in a full day and his thoughts were heavy. In addition, he was worried about Savannah and how the animosity between the two brothers would affect her. She was the one stuck in the middle between two angry men, struggling to maintain the peace. One brother was stubborn and unyielding, the other manipulative and demanding.

He wished there was some way he could protect her.

Twice Laredo had to ask Richard to turn out the light. "Give me five minutes," was the response both times. The light Laredo could handle; it was a small matter to turn on his side and put his back to the harsh glare. But the drunken singing and guitar strumming weren't as easily ignored.

By midnight he'd had enough. He threw back the covers, walked over to the wall and flicked off the switch himself. "You got a problem with that?" he challenged. His day had started at five that morning and he desperately needed to sleep.

A tense silence followed. "Whatever," Richard muttered. He dropped or shoved something onto the floor, and the crash echoed through the room. Frankly, Laredo didn't care. He was through with the niceties as far as Richard Weston was concerned.

Laredo awoke at dawn, showered, shaved and was preparing for his day when he happened to notice Richard. He stopped, squinting as he took a closer look. He'd heard movie stars and the like used such devices, but he'd never personally seen one.

Richard Weston lay sprawled across the bed, his arms and legs dangling over the edge of the small mattress. He wore silk pajamas and, of all things, a black satin sleep mask to protect his eyes against the sunlight. Never in all his life had Laredo seen a more incongruous sight in a bunkhouse.

Shaking his head, he stopped in the barn to check on Roanie before he made his way to the kitchen for coffee. Squatting down, he gently tested the roan's leg, working with practiced hands, exploring the damage to the delicate muscle. The swelling was down and the pain had apparently lessened.

After coffee and a solitary breakfast, Laredo worked in the rose garden; he installed the trellises he'd built earlier in the week and transplanted some shrubs Savannah wanted him to move. She hadn't come outside and he guessed she was still busy in the house. Actually he hoped she'd treat herself and sleep in. She must have been exhausted yesterday, cooking for her ungrateful brother. He gritted his teeth just thinking about the other man.

Shortly after noon Richard wandered out of the bunkhouse, looking as if he hadn't been awake more than a few minutes. His hair was mussed and he yawned as he strolled across the yard, his shirt unbuttoned. He wore canvas shoes without socks.

Before going to the house for lunch, Laredo decided to rewrap Roanie's leg and apply the ointment again. He was half-finished when he felt someone's presence. He turned around and found Grady standing outside the stall watching him.

"I understand I'm in your debt," he said with the pride of a man who preferred to owe no one. He looked tired and drawn, as if he hadn't slept much. For the first time since making Grady's acquaintance, Laredo felt sorry for him.

"No problem," he said, straightening. He rubbed his

hand down Roanie's back, reassuring the gelding that all was well.

Grady lingered. Apparently there was something else on his mind. "Savannah told you about the ghost town, didn't she?"

"She mentioned it," Laredo said stiffly.

"I thought she might have." Grady leaned against the stall door. "Listen, I haven't made my feelings any secret. I don't like you, Smith. Nor do I trust you. A man who steals gets no respect from me."

"For what it's worth, I didn't do it," Laredo said, although he doubted Grady would believe him.

"I have even less respect for a liar."

Laredo tensed. If it wasn't for Savannah, he'd have had his fist down the other man's throat. He'd worked hard to prove himself, but apparently a good day's labor wasn't enough for Grady Weston.

"You should know I've asked Sheriff Hennessey to do a background check on you, although I suspect Smith is probably an alias."

Laredo's hackles were already raised, but defending himself again would be a useless waste of breath. He exhaled sharply. "Fine. To be fair, if Savannah was my sister, I'd do the same thing. You're looking to protect her. I can't blame a man for that."

If Grady was surprised, he didn't show it.

"I'm pleased to hear you say that, because she needs protecting."

Savannah's brother had Laredo's attention now. "What do you mean?"

"Unfortunately she mentioned finding Bitter End to Richard and he seemed far too interested. I heard the bastard when I was washing up for dinner. He was hinting that she should take him there." He paused. "I don't want it to happen."

Laredo agreed with Grady. "She's already promised me she wouldn't return alone. I hope she doesn't go with Richard, either."

Surprise flickered in Grady's intensely blue eyes. "So she did plan to go back." He scratched the side of his head. "Why on earth would she do such a thing?" He looked to Laredo for the answer.

"The roses," he said, amazed Grady hadn't figured it out.

"She's already got more roses than she knows what to do with. How could she possibly want more? What's wrong with that woman? Why would she risk her fool neck over a few flowers?"

"She's after old roses," Laredo explained.

"Old roses." The two words were part of a deep sigh. Grady seemed lost in thought for a minute and then his gaze found Laredo's again. "I don't want her going there with Richard or anyone else, for that matter. It's not safe. Regardless of my feelings toward you, I care about my sister and I'd appreciate your help."

"You might find this hard to believe, Grady, but I care about Savannah's well-being, too."

"Then keep her away from Bitter End."

Laredo wasn't sure he could do that. "I'm not making any promises, but I'll do what I can."

Grady nodded wearily. "That's all I ask." He hesitated, glanced over at Roanie's leg and then back to Laredo. "We could use a wrangler this time of year. Are you interested in the job?"

"I'd need to square it with Savannah."

"That isn't what I asked," Grady said, his words sharp.

"I'm interested," Laredo answered.

"Fine," he said. "You can start after lunch."

DAMN, BUT THE OLD TOWN looked good. It was mid-afternoon as Richard slowly drove Grady's battered pickup down Main Street. He'd barely been back twenty-four hours, and it felt as if he'd never left. Well, not quite, but close enough. He'd thought about returning to Promise more than once—but not driving his brother's clunky truck.

Despite the town's familiarity, a lot had changed over the years. The savings-and-loan had a sign that alternately flashed the time and the temperature. Damn if that didn't beat all. Next thing he knew the town would have its own Dairy Queen.

Luck was with him. Slowly but surely he'd manage to wriggle his way back into Grady's good graces—enough, at any rate, to convince his big brother to let him stay for a while. It wouldn't take long to win Savannah back, but then his sister had always been a soft touch. Grady, however, wasn't nearly as easy. So far, it was Richard two, Grady zilch.

Because not only was Richard staying at the ranch, he had the truck. Okay, Savannah had been the one to give him the keys, but what Grady didn't know wasn't going to hurt him.

His brother was a fool. Grady could have sold that ranch ten times over and lived off the profits for years. Instead he'd half killed himself holding on to twenty thousand smelly cattle-filled acres. Richard had listened to the spiel about their forefathers struggling against impossible odds and all that garbage. So what? He wasn't about to let the ranch or anything else tie him down. He had better ideas than following a bunch of senseless cattle around all that godforsaken land.

Richard pulled into the first available parking spot and hopped out of the cab. Six years away, and he still knew this town inside out, recognized every street and practically every building. On the other hand, no one was going to recognize *him*, dressed as he was. What he needed, Richard decided, was new clothes.

His first stop was Jordan's Town and Country. Max Jordan who owned the place would be close to retirement by now.

"Max," Richard said as he walked into the Western-wear store. He greeted Max as if they'd been the best of friends, slapping the older man jovially on the back. "Don't you know me?" he asked. "Richard. Richard Weston."

"Richard." The other man's eyes brightened with recognition. "When did you get back?"

"Yesterday. Listen, does Grady still have an open account with you?" He fingered the pearl buttons on a polished-cotton shirt and checked the cost, raising his brows at the price.

"That's one of our designer shirts," Max said, and steered him toward another less pricy rack of clothes.

Richard returned to the original shirt. "Do you have it in a forty-two?"

"I think I just might," Max said with some surprise. He shifted hangers as he searched out sizes. "Yup, got one right here."

"Great. Grady said I should buy what I need."

"Not a problem," Max assured him, grinning at the prospect of a big sale. "How's Grady doing these days? I don't see much of him."

"He works too hard," Richard said. And it was true. His brother needed to relax and not take everything so seriously.

"It's good to see you, my boy," Max said, watching Richard try on a pair of three-hundred-dollar snakeskin boots. They fit perfectly, as if they were just waiting for him. "I'll take these, as well."

"Good choice."

Grady wouldn't think so, but Richard would pay him back. Eventually.

"I've got to say I still miss your parents," Max continued. "They were good people. My, but your mother knew how to cook, and your pa, why, he was the life of the party."

The word "party" struck a pleasant chord with Richard. He didn't imagine there'd been much celebrating around the Yellow Rose since he'd been away. Not with Grady being such a tightwad. He doubted his brother even knew how to laugh anymore, and Savannah ran and hid from her own shadow.

"Funny you should mention a party," Richard said as the owner tallied the bill. "Grady's throwing a bash to welcome me home on Sunday. You're welcome to come. Bring the missus too."

"Who else'll be there?"

"The whole town's invited. Spread the word, will you?"

"Sure. It'll be great for everyone to get together. Haven't had a real party all spring, and it's weeks yet until the big summer dance."

Richard left soon after signing his name to the yellow slip. On the sidewalk outside Jordan's he ran into Ellie Frasier. "Ellie," he said, and did a double take. "Little Ellie?" Only she wasn't so little anymore. She'd been in junior high when he was a high school senior, and he remembered thinking then that she was going to be a looker. He'd been right.

She stared at him blankly.

"Richard!" he cried, and spread his arms wide. He was surprised she didn't recognize him in his new shirt, hat and boots. He gaze lowered to her full breasts. He always had been partial to a well-endowed woman. Yup, he could see he'd come home in the nick of time. No ring on her finger, either. Not that it mattered. Often, forbidden fruit was all the sweeter.

"Richard Weston?"

"The one and only."

She asked the same questions as Max—when he'd arrived, what he'd been doing, how long he planned to stay and so on. He was vague until he mentioned the party.

"Bring whoever you want, but be sure to save me a dance, all right?" He winked, letting her know he was interested.

"I don't know... My dad's been sick and—"

"Come, anyway," he urged. "You need the break, and what better way to put your troubles behind you than to kick up your heels and party?"

Dancing. That meant music. They were going to need a band, and on short notice. That'd cost a few extra bucks, but hey, no problem. Grady was tight with a penny, but he probably had plenty of cash stored away. His older brother was too much like their father to cut it close to the bone.

"Who's playing at the Chili Pepper these days?" he asked, referring to the best barbecue pit in town.

Ellie named a band he hadn't heard of. He nodded and headed in that direction. While he was there, he'd arrange to have Adam Braunfels set up a barbecue. They were going to need lots of food. Naturally Savannah would want to cook up most of it herself, make salads and such; she'd insist on that the same way Mom would if she were alive.

He remembered his parents with fondness. Their deaths had put an unexpected crimp in his life, but Richard was a survivor. The years had proved that. He'd weathered his current troubles, hadn't he? He was home and as safe as a babe in arms.

By the time Richard drove back to the ranch, he'd made a number of arrangements for the party. He'd ordered a dozen cases of beer and he'd made sure there was going to be plenty of soda pop for the youngsters. Millie over at the flower shop had suggested Chinese lanterns and agreed to set them up early in the afternoon. For a price, naturally, but she'd been reasonable about it.

Savannah was working in her garden when he arrived. She wore one of those long dresses of hers with an oversize straw hat and looked more like a nun than the big sister he remembered. Briefly he wondered what was up between her and that prickly hired hand.

"My, don't you look beautiful this afternoon," Richard said as he waltzed through the gate. "As pretty as one of your roses."

She blushed and Richard was struck by how truly pretty she was. It surprised him.

"Listen, sis, I probably shouldn't have done this, but I ran into some friends in town."

Savannah straightened and dabbed the sweat from her brow. "I imagine everyone was glad to see you."

"They were, but there just wasn't enough time to visit with everyone the way I wanted. I hope you don't mind, but I invited a few people over for dinner Sunday evening. You wouldn't mind cooking up some of your prize-winning potato salad, now, would you?"

"For how many?"

Richard laughed and hugged her close. "Enough for about 150."

Chapter Six

Grady swore Richard must have invited the entire population of Promise to this so-called party. Neighbors and friends whirled around the makeshift dance floor, while others sat in the sunshine and exchanged gossip. Grady didn't want anything to do with it.

The first he'd heard of Richard's party was when he found Savannah in the kitchen this morning cooking her heart out. The next thing he knew, Millie Greenville from the local flower shop was stringing Chinese lanterns around the backyard and asking him when he intended to set up the tables. According to Millie, he was going to need at least twenty to accommodate everyone.

Before he fully comprehended what was happening, people started to arrive. The lead singer of the Hoss Cartrights asked him questions he couldn't answer. Apparently they didn't need his help because the next time he stepped out of the barn, they'd set up a stage, plugged in their sound equipment and spread a bale of straw across the lawn for a dance floor.

Richard, dressed in his fancy new duds, was in his element. Grady didn't know what had possessed him to give in to Savannah's pleadings to let their worthless brother stay on until his severance check showed up.

Grady wasn't entirely convinced there *was* a check. Furthermore he wondered where the hell Richard was getting the money to pay for his new clothes, not to mention this party. The guy was supposed to be broke. Well, maybe he had a chargecard he hadn't told them about.

As for Richard's staying on, Savannah insisted it'd only be a few days. Richard needed to recuperate, rest up. To hear her tell it, you'd think he'd been working on a chain gang for the past six years and was practically at death's door. Judging by the energy his kid brother displayed on the dance floor, he'd recovered quickly, Grady thought.

The beer flowed free and easy. Grady was on his second bottle himself: The Chili Pepper's spicy barbecue sauce sizzled on the large tin-drum grills, filling the air with a spicy smoky aroma. The dinner line extended halfway around the house.

Those who weren't eating or dancing mingled in the yard, making themselves at home. Grady had originally decided not to participate in Richard's party, but his standoffishness hadn't lasted long.

Cal and Glen Patterson, neighboring ranchers and friends, arrived then. They sat with him on the porch steps. Grady couldn't remember the last time he'd shot the breeze with the brothers. The three of them had grown up together and remained close to this day. As close as Grady allowed anyone to get.

"I didn't think you'd ever welcome Richard back," Cal said, leaning back, a beer in one hand. Cal and the sheriff were the only two who knew about Richard's theft. It wasn't the kind of information you shared about family.

"I didn't welcome him back." Grady wanted that understood right then and there. This party wasn't his idea.

Grady noticed Sheriff Hennessey twirling Dovie Boyd around the dance floor. His opinion of the lawman had fallen several degrees when he'd failed to turn up anything on Smith. If the man was doing his job, he grumbled to himself, Frank would be down at the office right this minute, instead of partying.

"If you aren't responsible for this welcoming, then whose idea was it?" Cal asked. "Savannah's?"

"Nope. Richard organized it himself." Grady took another swallow of beer. The cold brew helped relieve his growing sense of frustration. Again he wondered how Richard intended to pay for all this. Surely he wasn't expecting *him* to foot the bill. That would be too brazen even for Richard.

His mistake, Grady realized, was giving in and allowing Richard to stay that first night. Now his younger brother had manipulated him once again—made it look as if Grady had welcomed him back with open arms. As far as he was concerned, Richard couldn't leave soon enough.

Savannah had been slaving in the kitchen since before dawn. Neighbors he hadn't seen in months had brought over pies, cakes and an assortment of side dishes; they'd delivered picnic tables and dozens of lawn chairs. And now Grady was indebted to each and every one of them. His neighbors would be looking for return favors, too. Especially of the social kind. It wouldn't take long for the invites to arrive, and he'd be expected to accept. Damn it all. He'd never been a party goer and didn't intend to start now.

"What I'd like to know," Grady muttered to his friends, "is how the hell he's paying for all this."

"Did you ask him?" Glen, the younger of the Patterson brothers, inquired.

"I didn't have a chance." The party was happening before Grady even knew there was going to be one. If he'd had a clue what his brother was up to, he would have put a stop to it. The last time he'd seen this many people had been the day he buried his parents. Leave it to Richard to dredge up the most pain-filled memory of his life.

"Who's that?" Glen asked, directing their attention to a blond woman walking in from the driveway. The row of cars stretched all the way to the road. Fifty at last count.

Grady didn't recognize the newcomer, either. She was young and pretty, if such attributes mattered to him, which they didn't. She didn't seem to know many people because she stood at the edge of the crowd, looking self-conscious in a pin-striped power suit. Whoever she was, she'd completely overdressed for the party.

Cal sat up and gave her a long stare. "Isn't that the new doc? Jane something-or-other."

"She's a doctor?" Glen asked with disbelief. "Promise has a lady doctor? When did all this happen?"

"Last week." Cal nudged his brother with an elbow. "Don't you two read the paper?"

"Who has time?" Grady wanted to know.

"Cal keeps the weekly edition by the john, don't you, big brother?" Glen teased.

"Well, it gets read, doesn't it?" Cal chided. "Her picture was on the front page. She's here on one of those government programs."

"What government program?"

"I don't know the name of it, but the paper said she agreed to work off her medical-school loans by volunteering her skill in a deprived area."

"Promise is a deprived area?" This was news to Grady.

"Must be," Cal muttered, sounding as surprised as Grady.

"Hey, we got a doctor who didn't fight in the battle for the Alamo?"

Doc Cummings had retired at the first of the year at the age of seventy. At least he admitted to being seventy, but in Grady's opinion, he was on the shady side of that figure. He'd delivered Grady and just about everyone else in town under forty. Rumor had it that Doc Cummings was lazing his days away on the Gulf coast now, eating shrimp and soaking up the sunshine. Grady wished the old coot well.

Caroline Daniels strolled past, carrying a bowl of potato salad. She returned a minute or so later with an empty one. Straining, Grady glanced into the kitchen and caught a glimpse of Savannah feverishly making another batch of salad. Smith was there with her, sitting at the table and dutifully peeling potatoes. Those two were as thick as thieves, despite all his warnings. His talk with Laredo Smith hadn't made any difference; he suspected Savannah was still planning a return visit to Bitter End. It hadn't been easy swallowing his pride and asking for Smith's help. The wrangler appeared to have gotten the wrong message, too, because he spent every available minute with Savannah, just as if Grady had given the pair his blessing. He hadn't. Despite his job offer, he wanted the other man off the ranch and the sooner the better.

"Are you going to dance with me or not?" Breathlessly Ellie Frasier plopped herself down next to Glen. They were good friends and had been for years. Grady had never understood how a man could be friends with a woman and not get romantically involved. But that seemed to be the way it was with Glen and Ellie. They were friends and nothing more.

Ellie needed a confidant these days, according to Cal. Her father was terminally ill and had been transferred to a hospital in San Antonio. Her mother was spending all her time there while Ellie ran the family store. Grady sympathized; he knew all too well the pain of losing a parent. Ellie was young to be taking on such heavy responsibility, but from what he heard, she was up to the task. She spent as much time as possible visiting her father, and between driving to San Antonio and managing the business, she was running herself ragged. It surprised him a little that Ellie was at the party, and he guessed Glen had something to do with that. Getting away from all the emotional pressures was probably the best thing for her.

"So what about that dance, Patterson?"

"Seems to me you've already got yourself a dance partner," Glen said. He stared pointedly in Richard's direction. Grady's brother was at his most charming, teasing and laughing with the women, exchanging jokes with the men. Outgoing, personable, the life of the party—and self-appointed guest of honor, to boot.

"I gotta say," Ellie said, speaking to Grady, "your brother's mighty light on his feet."

Yeah, in more ways than one. Grady was tempted to say it but didn't. He frowned, instead. Richard had been on the dance floor for hours without revealing any signs of slowing down. Grady suspected his brother had danced with every woman in town at least once, and the pretty ones twice. He'd taken a liking to Ellie, that was for sure. Grady had seen the two of them dancing three or four times already. He wanted to issue a word of caution, seeing how vulnerable Ellie must be feeling, but he bit his tongue. She'd find out soon enough what kind of man his brother was.

"I'd forgotten how much fun Richard could be," Ellie said.

"He's a regular laugh fest," Grady agreed sarcastically; he couldn't help it. Ellie studied him for a moment and he hoped she'd gotten the message.

"Don't mind Grady," Glen said, looping his arm around Ellie's shoulders. "He's just sore because he doesn't have anyone to dance with."

Grady's frown deepened. He wasn't about to make a fool of himself in front of the entire town. While Richard might know his way around a dance floor, Grady had been cursed with two left feet. The last time he'd attempted to dance he'd been in his teens and forced to wear a suit and boutonniere.

"I haven't seen this many people since the Willie Nelson Fourth of July picnic," Cal said. Like Grady, his friend wasn't much of a social animal. Glen was by far the most outgoing of the three men. He'd tried to drag Grady off to the town's biggest function—next to the cattlemen's dance and the rodeo—for the past six years. Every Fourth of July Promise threw a Willie Nelson picnic, hoping the popular entertainer would agree to visit. Willie had politely declined each year, but the town councillors hadn't let that deter them from holding the affair in the singer's honor.

"Come on," Ellie urged, tugging at Glen's hand. "I want to dance." With a show of reluctance, Glen untangled his feet and stood.

The pair were out of earshot when Cal spoke. "We won't see him the rest of the night. Once he's out on the floor, he won't quit."

"Go ahead if you feel like it," Grady told his friend. "No need to keep me company."

"No thanks. I'm happy to sit here for a while."

Cal lingered an hour or so, not that they said much. This was what Grady enjoyed most about his friend. They didn't have to fill every silence with idle chatter. A couple of times he was on the verge of mentioning Savannah's recent trek to the ghost town, but he held his tongue. The last time either one of them had talked about Bitter End, they'd been in their teens. Anyway, there wasn't anything Cal could tell him he didn't already know. Besides, Savannah was his concern, not his neighbor's. After a time Cal drifted away to get himself some barbecue.

Laughter and music abounded. It disgusted Grady to watch his brother. Richard continued to be sociable and entertaining, the focus of the party. It certainly hadn't taken him long to put the good people of Promise under his spell. Once again Grady wondered how his brother intended to pay for all this, but it wasn't his concern, and he wasn't going to worry about it.

The kitchen door opened and Caroline stepped outside. Her gaze caught Grady's; she waved, then walked over to where Adam Braunfels was handing out beer. She collected two.

Grady was somewhat surprised when she brought the extra bottle over to him. "You look like you could use this," she said, and sat down on the step beside him. She tucked one knee under her chin while her foot tapped to the beat of the music.

Grady saluted her with the bottle and took a long swallow of beer. Neither spoke for a few minutes; both of them just stared at the dance floor. Finally Caroline said, "He's really something, isn't he?"

"If you came over here to sing Richard's praises, I don't want to hear them."

"This might surprise you, Grady, but I'm not a fan of your brother's."

It *was* news to Grady, and he found himself grateful that at least one other person hadn't been blinded by Richard's charm. "I get the impression you aren't particularly fond of me, either," he said wryly.

She grinned. "I don't dislike you. I don't always agree with you, but you're not half-bad."

It wasn't much of a compliment, but Grady would take what he could get. "Hey, careful. Sweet talk just might turn my head."

Caroline burst into laughter.

Grady smiled for probably the first time that day. "So you're not one of Richard's adoring fans." Funny how that one bit of information encouraged him.

"If it was up to me, I'd string Richard up by his thumbs. Savannah's been stuck in the kitchen for hours. I don't think she had any idea what to expect. Richard had told her to plan for about 150 people—she assumed he was joking."

Right then and there Grady decided that, come morning, Richard was off the Yellow Rose. He didn't care how many arguments Savannah made in their brother's defense. They should've run him off the property the minute he set foot on their land. Grady shook his head. Surely Savannah would agree with him now.

"Maggie certainly seems to be taken with him," he noted, frowning as he brought the beer bottle to his lips. His younger brother danced with the five-year-old, twirling her about the floor. The youngster's shrieks of delight could be heard over the music. Richard's success with Maggie rankled, especially since the child ran away in terror whenever she laid eyes on Grady. Somehow or other, without realizing what he'd done, Grady had frightened the kid. For the life of him, he didn't know how it'd happened, and despite his efforts, he hadn't been able to repair the damage.

Caroline kept a close watch on her daughter. "She's easily swayed by charm, it seems."

"She isn't the only one."

"Are you jealous, Grady?"

"Hell, no," he protested before he had a chance to fully consider the question. On second thought, he had to admit there was a grain of truth in Caroline's words.

It was bad enough that Richard had implied—or outright said—that Grady and Savannah were throwing him this party. The fact that he had just about every woman in town fawning over him and almost every man eager for his company only added insult to injury.

"I don't suppose I could convince you to take a spin," Caroline said, motioning with her head toward the dance floor.

"Not on your life."

Caroline sighed as though disappointed. "That's what I thought."

"Hey, you don't need me." He gestured toward a group of single men standing under a live oak tree. "Any one of them would be happy to dance with you."

"I suppose." But she didn't budge and, truth be known, he was glad she didn't. He thought of inviting her to go bowling with him—that would be more to his liking—but hesitated. It'd been so damn long since he'd gone out on a date he wasn't sure how to go about asking.

Then it dawned on Grady that maybe Caroline was interested in him. "Are you saying you want to dance with *me?*" In other circumstances he probably wouldn't have asked, but he'd downed three beers on an almost empty stomach and his inhibitions were definitely lowered.

"I might be," she responded.

He mulled over her answer. He liked Caroline, admired her for the good friend she was to Savannah, and while he'd certainly noticed her, found her attractive, he'd never thought to make anything of it.

"You should get married," he said, and for the life of him, Grady didn't know what had prompted him to suggest such a thing. Horrified, he stared down at his empty beer bottle.

"Do you have anyone in mind?" Caroline asked.

"Not me." He wanted that understood.

"Don't worry, Grady, you aren't in the running."

He'd asked for that, but he didn't like hearing it. Then, thinking he should resolve this before things got out of hand, he decided to explain. "Maggie needs a father."

Caroline was on her feet so fast it made his head spin. "Don't tell me what my daughter needs or doesn't need, Grady."

"Fine, I won't."

"Good," she declared, and stomped away.

Women! They had to have the last word. But after Caroline left, Grady regretted the conversation. Worse, he knew he was one hundred percent at fault. He should never have said the things he had. It wasn't his place to suggest Maggie needed a father. It had made him sound judgmental or disapproving when that wasn't his intent at all. He respected Caroline; he just thought her life as a working single mother was too hard. And he hated the way little Maggie seemed so susceptible to any man's charm. Any *con* man's charm. Well, nothing he could do about it now.

The sun set and after a while someone lit the Chinese lanterns. The lights swayed in a soft breeze, casting shadows that danced about the yard. The band switched from lively melodies and line dances to slower, more mellow songs. Couples, wrapped in each other's arms, slowly circled the floor.

Families with young children packed up their youngsters and started home, prompted by thoughts of work and school in the morning. Playing the role of gracious host to a T, Richard escorted them to their cars, then stood in the driveway and waved them off.

"Nice party," Adam Braunfels said as Grady headed toward the house, around nine o'clock.

"Not *my* party," he was quick to tell the owner of Chili Pepper.

"I hope everything was satisfactory," Adam said next.

Grady tucked his hands in his back pockets. "Great. I certainly didn't hear any complaints."

"Good. I want you to know I was as fair as I could be with the tally."

Grady didn't know what Adam was talking about or, rather, why Adam was telling *him*, but he nodded his head, which had started to pound. He hadn't eaten since breakfast and his mind continued to dwell on his disastrous conversation with Caroline.

Adam pulled a slip of paper from his hip pocket and handed it to Grady. "I'd appreciate if you could write me a check now, Grady, before I go back to town."

"What?" He was sure there'd been some mistake.

"For the barbecue," Adam explained as if he were dense. Grady knew why he wanted to be paid; what he didn't understand was why Adam expected *him* to do it.

"I already said this wasn't my party."

Adam's mouth thinned. "I don't care whose party it is, I need my money."

"And you expect me to pay?"

"Yes."

"This is Richard's business." Grady was about to walk off when Richard raced to their side.

"I need my money," Adam repeated, looking from one brother to the other.

Richard's feet shifted nervously. "Would you mind paying him, Grady?" he asked. "I honestly thought my check would be here before now." He looked down at his boots. "I...I feel horrible about this."

Arms folded, Adam stared at Grady, ignoring Richard completely.

Grady felt as though the top of his head was about to explode. He had no choice but to pay up. His brother had done it to him again. Either he wrote Adam a check now or he came off looking like the bad guy.

LAREDO WAS ELBOW-DEEP in the kitchen sink when Frank Hennessey walked into the room. The sheriff nodded politely at Savannah, who sat with her feet propped up on a chair. It was the first time all day Laredo could get her to take a break. He knew she was exhausted. Hell, he was himself, and he hadn't worked near as hard as she had.

While he hadn't been particularly fond of Richard before, Laredo actively disliked him now. He'd been around men like the younger Weston in his time. Fast talkers. Users. Selfish and thoughtless. Richard certainly knew which buttons to push when it came to his sister, Laredo had noticed. All he had to do was mention their mother, and Savannah crumbled. It infuriated him to watch the jerk take advantage of her that way.

Laredo knew Grady was on to Richard, but he suspected Savannah wasn't. Even if she did find out what kind of man her brother was, she was perfectly capable of overlooking it, and that worried Laredo.

"If you don't mind, Mr. Smith, I've got a few questions I'd like to ask you," the sheriff said.

A little confused, Laredo lifted his hands from the dishwater and reached for a towel. He didn't like the idea of the sheriff singling him out, but he didn't want to make a fuss in front of Savannah, either.

"Is there a problem, Sheriff?" Savannah asked, looking concerned.

"No, no." Hennessey caught Laredo's glance. "Perhaps you'd like to step outside, Mr. Smith."

"Sure." Laredo dried his hands and squelched his growing sense of irritation. Grady had put the lawman up to this; he'd admitted it earlier himself. Not that Laredo had anything to hide, but he hated the way it made him look to Savannah.

He waited until they were in the cool night air before he spoke. "I don't have any kind of record."

"Wrong," the lawman was quick to correct him. "You ran a red light back in 1995."

Stuffing his hands in his back hip pockets, Laredo glared at the sheriff. "I stand corrected."

Hennessey ignored the sarcasm. "I got a couple of questions for you."

"Fire away." Laredo clamped his teeth together, anger simmering.

"How long do you plan to stay in Promise?"

"As long as I damn well please." His tolerance for this kind of treatment was gone.

"Listen, Smith, it won't do you any good to get smart-mouthed with me. If you want trouble, you don't need to look any farther than right here. I can make enough trouble to last you a lifetime. Now I suggest you check your attitude.'' He gave him a moment to let the warning take hold, then repeated the question.

"I plan on heading out as soon as I can pay for the repairs to my truck." Laredo kept his voice a monotone and trained his gaze on the barn door.

The lawman's crisp voice mellowed when he next spoke. "Miss Savannah's a mighty fine woman."

Laredo's eyes clashed with the sheriff's. "You think I don't know that?"

"No one wants to see her hurt."

"I don't, either," Laredo said. He didn't understand why everyone assumed he'd purposely do anything to hurt Savannah.

"For reasons I can't quite grasp, she seems to have taken a liking to you. But if you're leaving soon, I figure you'll be gone before there's any real damage done."

Laredo kept his mouth shut, knowing the lawman would use anything he said against him.

"Look, I know I'm speaking out of turn here, Smith. It's none of my affair when you come or go. All I'm saying is that a lot of folks around here think highly of Savannah. No one wants to see her used, especially by a drifter who'll desert her without a second thought. You get what I'm saying?"

Laredo pressed his lips tightly closed in order to hold his tongue.

"Good. Like I said, Savannah's the sweetest gentlest soul in these parts, and if you or anyone else decides to take advantage of her, you'll answer directly to me. You got that, boy?"

Laredo's shoulders ached because of the stiff way he held his back. It'd been a lot of years since anyone had

called him "boy." Laredo hadn't liked it then and liked
it even less now.

"You heard me?" Sheriff Hennessey asked, more
forcefully this time.

"Loud and clear."

The lawman nodded and slapped Laredo amiably on
the shoulder. "I'm glad we had this little talk. Now you
go back to whatever you were doing, and I'll give Miss
Dovie one last spin around the dance floor."

Laredo didn't comment. He stood rigid and angry
while the sheriff strolled away.

"Laredo?" Savannah said his name softly as she
joined him. "Is there a problem?" The distress in her
voice melted away his anger. Hennessey was only speaking his mind, prompted, of course, by Grady. The long
hours he'd spent working with Roanie hadn't been
enough to prove himself to Savannah's brother. But Laredo didn't imagine Grady was ever going to accept him,
no matter what he did. Not that it was necessary, other
than to ease Savannah's mind. The situation weighed
heavily on her, and for that reason alone, it bothered Laredo.

"Everything's fine," he told her.

"You sure?"

"Positive." He took her hand and led her to the porch
swing, then sat down beside her. After a few moments
he slipped his arm around her shoulders and she rested
her head against his chest. To hell with Grady Weston,
Laredo decided. He was holding Savannah and he didn't
give a damn *what* her older brother thought.

Despite his defiant attitude, Laredo had taken the sheriff at his word. Hennessey could easily make trouble for
him. He wasn't looking to cause problems, but he wasn't

going to run off with his tail dragging between his legs, either.

Savannah was quiet, and after a moment he assumed she'd gone to sleep. Content to hold her, Laredo entertained himself by watching the party, which was still in progress, although the numbers had dwindled considerably. He figured things must be winding down.

When the band took a break before their final set, Richard brought out his guitar. Taking advantage of the more or less captive audience, he started playing. A dozen people gathered around him. A few children, including Maggie, camped at his feet. A sing-along ensued, and Richard performed several of the songs he'd massacred a few nights earlier in the bunkhouse. Only this time he managed to do a respectable job of carrying a tune, and the words were recognizable.

Twenty minutes later the band returned, and the lead singer encouraged all the men to bring their sweethearts onto the floor. Laredo watched as Richard chose Ellie Frasier—and even managed to steal a kiss when he thought no one was looking. He didn't dance with Ellie long, though, changing partners and dancing with several elderly ladies and then with Maggie and a few of the other children still at the party. The little girls' delight at having the guest of honor pay them such attention sounded in their excited shrieks. The guy was smooth, Laredo gave him that.

"Is this the sweetheart dance?" Savannah asked him, lifting her head from his shoulder.

"That's what he said."

She sighed deeply. Laredo had never been much of a ladies' man, but he knew what that sigh meant. Savannah wanted to dance the sweetheart dance with him, but she wouldn't ask. He had to be the one to invite her.

Damn, he wasn't any good at this romance stuff, but he hated to disappoint Savannah. Nor was he good at dancing. It always made him feel awkward and uncomfortable. Especially in front of an audience. And especially when it was this slow music.

Rather than disillusion her, though, Laredo stood and extended his hand in a courtly fashion. "May I have the honor of this dance?"

Her responding smile was worth any embarrassment he might bring on himself, Laredo decided. Savannah's beautiful blue eyes filled with happiness. "Does this mean I'm your sweetheart, Laredo Smith?" she asked softly.

Hennessey's words of warning echoed in his ears. But hell, the man could arrest him for all he cared just then. "It must."

Savannah placed her hand in his and stood.

"Be warned, I might step on your foot," he muttered under his breath as they approached the dance floor.

"I suggest you watch your own feet. It's been a long time since I did anything like this."

Laredo should have known Savannah would find a way to put him at ease. Being with her always made him feel...special. As though he alone, of all men, was worthy of this good and beautiful woman. Right this minute he could almost believe it....

Several couples swayed to the romantic music, holding each other close. One couple was deeply involved in a kiss.

Laredo drew her into his arms and concentrated on moving his feet in a box step, mentally counting to four. One step back, one step to the right, one step forward and then to the left.

"Laredo," she whispered in his ear, wrapping her arms around his neck. "Relax, okay?"

"But—"

"All I really wanted was for you to hold me."

That was all he wanted, too. He shut his eyes and pulled her into the shadows. He kissed her ear, smiling when he felt her shiver.

"Like that, do you?"

"Oh, yes."

He rubbed her back.

"I like that, too."

Laredo was just beginning to feel that he had the hang of this when she captured his earlobe between her lips and gently sucked on it. His eyes flew open and his blood went hot. He slowly let the breath drain from his lungs, then locked his hands at the small of her back. Soon she was flush against him. With her softness touching him like that, in the most intimate places, Laredo lost count of the steps. Not long afterward, he discontinued dancing altogether, other than to shuffle his feet a little.

"Laredo," she whispered. "I'm glad Grady asked you to stay. I'm glad for a lot of reasons."

"Me, too," he whispered. "So glad…"

The song continued and he closed his eyes again, wanting to savor these moments. His heart felt so full it actually hurt. Until now, with Savannah in his embrace, Laredo hadn't thought such a possibility existed. But his heart ached. Not with grief or pain but with love.

Of all the memories that could have come to him at a time like this, the one that did was of his father. The last memory he had of his father still alive.

Laredo had been a young boy when his father left for Vietnam. He didn't understand about war; all he knew was that the man he adored was going away. He'd hidden in the barn, thinking if no one could find him, maybe his father wouldn't have to leave. Naturally his childish plan hadn't worked, and he'd been found in short order.

Then his dad had taken him on his lap and held him for a long time without saying a word. When he did speak, he'd promised Laredo that, no matter what happened while he was away, nothing—not distance, not time, not even death—would separate Laredo from his father's love.

Months later, when Laredo had stood in front of a cold casket and watched his father's body lowered into the ground, he'd recalled those words. At the memorial service he'd stood proud and tall. His mother and grandparents had wept, overcome with grief, but Laredo's eyes had remained dry.

Emotion welled up inside him now and he understood, perhaps for the first time, the intensity of the love his parents had shared. The depth of it. With this revelation came the knowledge that he felt the same way about Savannah. His mother had never remarried, and Laredo finally understood why.

A gruff voice broke into his thoughts and he lifted his head from Savannah's to see her older brother standing by the side of the dance floor.

"I don't like the way you're holding my sister."

Laredo released Savannah. Grady Weston's face was flushed and angry.

"Grady, please!" Savannah reluctantly moved away from Laredo. "You're making a scene and embarrassing me."

"Leave us alone," Laredo warned. Their eyes met, challenged, clashed. His willingness to make peace with Grady had vanished after that talk with the sheriff.

Before he realized exactly how it had happened, he and Grady were facing off, their fists raised.

"Grady, stop!" Savannah cried, and when it did no good, she turned to Laredo. "If you care for me, you won't do this."

Laredo did care, so damn much it terrified him. But this was one fight he wasn't walking away from.

"Please," Savannah said, stepping directly in front of him.

Laredo felt himself weakening.

Caroline Daniels arrived then and slid her arm through Grady's. "It seems to me that what you need is a nice hot cup of coffee," she announced, steering him toward the kitchen.

Laredo watched the two of them walk toward the house.

Savannah slipped her arms back around Laredo's neck. "I believe this dance was mine," she said, nestling close to him once more.

A lot more than this dance belonged to Savannah Weston, Laredo realized. She also owned his heart.

Chapter Seven

The early-morning sun shone cheerfully on the Yellow Rose. Savannah had been much too tired the night before to worry about cleanup, but in the revealing light of day, the entire front yard was a disaster. The Chinese lanterns sagged. Paper plates and napkins littered the once-flawless grass amid a welter of abandoned tables and chairs. The straw from the dance area stretched like a spider web from one end of the lawn to the other.

While the coffee brewed, Savannah dragged a garbage can into the yard. She'd only been working ten or fifteen minutes when Grady joined her. Wiley and Laredo followed, yawning. Savannah quickly distributed plastic garbage bags, since there was far too much trash for one container.

"Where's Richard?" Grady demanded.

"Sleeping," Wiley said with a chuckle. "What did you expect?" He began picking up litter and stuffing it into a bag.

"Then drag his sorry ass out here. It was his party. The least he can do is clean up the mess he created."

"Why should he start now?" Again the question came from Wiley.

"I got better things to do than this," Grady grumbled, stuffing his own armload of garbage into a bag.

"I didn't hire on to do housekeeping, either," the foreman put in.

Savannah had heard enough. "Stop it—both of you!" she shouted, unable to bear the bickering. It was rare for her to raise her voice, let alone yell, and she immediately got everyone's attention. Grady and Wiley stopped and stared at her; even Rocket lifted his head, as if shocked by her outburst.

A frown creasing his brow, Laredo paused in his raking and waited.

"I didn't ask for your help," she said. "If you're going to complain, then leave. I'd rather tend to the cleanup myself than be subjected to your foul moods." The comment was directed at Grady. Her good feeling about her brother—the fact that he'd hired Laredo—was rapidly fading.

"I'm in one hell of a fine mood," Grady barked, grimacing in a parody of a smile. "I'm as happy as can be." Savannah thought he looked like he was posing for the cover of *Mad* magazine, but restrained herself from saying so.

"You're happy?" Wiley asked, his words drenched with sarcasm. "You look about as happy as when you wrote out that check to Adam Braunfels for the barbecue."

This was the first Savannah had heard about it. "Why'd you pay Adam?"

"I didn't have any choice," Grady snapped. "He wanted his money and Sleeping Beauty in there—" he gestured at the bunkhouse "—didn't have it. What the hell else could I do?"

Savannah wished she hadn't asked, since the money

was obviously a sore spot with Grady. Not that she blamed him, but surely Richard expected his check soon, otherwise he wouldn't have thrown himself this party.

"It was good of you to pay Adam," she said, wanting Grady to know she appreciated his dilemma. "Money's tight just now."

"My money got even tighter with the party," Grady muttered. "I hope to hell he doesn't expect me to pay for everything, because I won't do it." He sounded as though he wasn't sure who he was trying to convince, her or himself.

"Richard will make good on it," Savannah felt obliged to say. Her younger brother had made plenty of mistakes, but he'd learned his lesson. At least that was what he claimed—and what she desperately wanted to believe.

Although the party had drained her physically and emotionally, she'd enjoyed watching Richard with their neighbors. He'd been a gracious host, warm and welcoming, and it gave her a sense of pride. He was like their father in that way—although admittedly not in others.

Mel Weston had always been the life of the party. Friendly, charming, universally loved. Her world had gone dark without him there—to call her his princess, to give her encouragement and approval and unconditional love. Having Richard home again produced a flood of happy memories and she didn't want those destroyed. Not if she could help it. So she was willing to give him the benefit of the doubt.

Everyone had mentioned what fun Richard was and how the children had adored him, especially Maggie. Seeing them together had done Savannah's heart good. The five-year-old tended to shy away from men, but she'd taken to Richard at first meeting, and he'd been wonderful with her, paying her lots of attention.

"I kissed that money goodbye the minute I signed the check," Grady grumbled, telling her in no uncertain terms that he continued to distrust Richard.

"He'll pay you back," Savannah insisted.

Grady stared at her long enough to make her uncomfortable. "When are you going to learn, Savannah? What's it going to take? Richard's a user. He'll never amount to anything because he's never been made accountable. I want him off this ranch, understand?"

"You're wrong, Grady. Richard might have a few bad habits—we all do—but he has a good heart. I refuse to believe otherwise."

"Don't kid yourself. As soon as he's awake, I want him to pack up and leave. I've paid his debts for the last time."

"You don't mean that!" Savannah couldn't believe her brother could be so hard.

"I want him gone by noon."

"Grady...please." Her voice cracked with emotion. "Don't do this."

"I'm not giving in to you this time," Grady said, stuffing more garbage deep into the plastic bag.

Savannah jumped at the fierce anger she heard in him.

"Don't talk to her like that," Laredo demanded, walking over to Savannah. The animosity between him and Grady was worse than ever, Savannah knew. She had no idea what had possessed her brother to cause a scene on the dance floor.

In a replay of last night Laredo and Grady glared at each other with mutual dislike.

"What do you suggest we do?" Wiley asked her, apparently finding the men's behavior amusing. "Get a hose and cool 'em both down?"

"That doesn't sound like a bad idea," Savannah responded, grateful for his sense of humor in this tense situation.

"Okay." Wiley took charge. "We're done here," he said, stepping directly in front of Laredo.

Savannah thought Laredo might challenge the foreman, but after a short hesitation he nodded and set aside the rake. As he turned to head for the barn, he caught her watching him and winked.

Savannah blushed with pleasure, remembering the dance they'd shared. After spending all day and most of the evening in the kitchen, her hair damp with sweat and her clothes spattered with mustard and mayonnaise, she must have looked a sight. Yet he'd called her his sweetheart and looked at her as if she were beautiful. Savannah had always known she was no beauty. She'd never been one to turn men's heads, and being shy had made it worse.

Over time she'd given up hope she'd ever find love. She'd never felt real attraction for a man, and as far as she knew, had never inspired it, either. All these years she'd been certain that a husband and family were for others and not for her. Her roses and her pets had become like her children. Grady constantly complained about the way she spoiled Rocket, but the dog was old, and if he was more comfortable in the house, she had no objection to letting him inside. And although Grady complained, she noticed that he was as guilty as she was about sneaking him leftovers.

Her musings returned to Laredo, and her heart softened at the thought of him. In less than two weeks, he'd changed her life, given her reason to dream, given her the most precious of human emotions—hope.

She loved him. It was that simple. That profound.

"I suppose you're waiting for me to apologize for making an ass of myself last night," Grady said, breaking into her thoughts. She'd almost forgotten he was there.

"You owe Laredo and me an apology."

He paused, then to her amazement, agreed with her. "I suppose I do. My only excuse is that I was furious with Richard and took it out on Laredo. I realize I acted like an idiot. I don't have any excuse other than I'd been drinking on an empty stomach."

The irony of it, Savannah mused, was that Grady had ended up paying for a dinner he hadn't bothered to taste.

"I'd be obliged if we could put the incident behind us," he said stiffly.

"On one condition."

He held up his hand to stop her. "I already know. You want me to apologize to Laredo."

"You didn't start this morning any better than you left off last night."

"I know." He wiped a hand down his face and she noticed that his eyes were tired and sad, and she wondered if he'd gotten any sleep whatsoever. "I'll talk to him later."

"What do you have against him?" she asked, genuinely curious. "Laredo isn't anything like you think. He's thoughtful and hardworking and—"

"Do you mind if I listen to you sing his praises some other time?" Grady asked from between clenched teeth.

"Oh, Grady." It was then she realized her brother was suffering from a hangover. After his confrontation with Laredo, he'd apparently continued drinking—and probably not beer, either. The first moment she could Savannah had escaped to her room, taken a quick shower and fallen into bed. She'd fallen asleep immediately but woke periodically throughout the night. At least tired was all she felt—not hung over, like Grady.

"Yeah," he groaned. "I had a few drinks after everyone went home. Figured it'd calm me down. It didn't. But guess what? I found there was booze missing—my good single-malt Scotch. Where do you think it went?"

Savannah shook her head.

"Starts with 'R.'"

"Oh, no. Are you *sure?*"

Grady gave her a cynical look and returned to his garbage collecting.

When the cleanup was finished, Grady grabbed a cup of coffee and headed about his day; Savannah went back to the house. It was almost eleven before Richard bothered to make an appearance.

"Good morning, my beautiful Savannah!" He kissed her noisily on the cheek, then hopped onto the kitchen counter, bare feet dangling while he nursed a mug of coffee. "What's for breakfast?"

"It's almost time for lunch."

He didn't react. "I was looking forward to sampling some of those fluffy scrambled eggs of yours. I woke up dreaming about eggs all gooey with melted cheese and toasted homemade bread."

"Richard," she said, angry with him and needing to let him know, "how could you have left Grady to pay Mr. Braunfels for the barbecue?"

"I feel really bad about that. I explained the situation to Adam earlier, and he seemed okay with me paying when I could. I wonder what happened to make him change his mind."

She wanted so much to believe Richard, but it was becoming more and more difficult.

He must have realized that, because he leaped down off the counter, crossed the room and reached for her hand. "Savannah," he said, holding her gaze, "I promise you by everything I hold dear that I'll reimburse Grady the minute my check arrives. You've got to trust me."

She wanted to, but the doubts refused to go away.

"You're the only one who believes in me," Richard said in obvious distress. "If it wasn't for you, Grady would have kicked me off the ranch that first day. Give me this opportunity to prove myself, that's all I'm asking."

Savannah studied her brother, hoping against hope that he'd fulfill his promises.

The beginnings of a smile lit up his eyes. "I can hardly wait to see the look on Grady's face when I give him the money. Won't he be shocked?" He laughed as if viewing the scene that very moment.

Savannah relaxed. Richard was her brother. He'd made mistakes, painful ones, but he was older now, mature. He couldn't help his impulsive sociable nature—couldn't resist throwing that party. However, he wouldn't take advantage of her and Grady a second time, she was sure of it.

"Do you believe me?" The color of his eyes intensified as his gaze implored her to give him the benefit of the doubt.

Savannah couldn't refuse him. "I believe you," she whispered, and silently prayed he wouldn't let her down.

Richard squeezed her hand. "You won't be sorry, Savannah, I promise you. I'm going to prove Grady all wrong, just you wait and see. Then you can say 'I told you so' to our high-and-mighty brother. You trusted me when no one else would, and someday you'll be able to laugh in Grady's face."

"I'd never do that." Her older brother might be strong-willed and opinionated, but his intentions were good.

"Are you going to scramble me up some of my favorite cheese eggs?" he asked in a cajoling voice.

She'd finished washing the breakfast dishes fifteen minutes earlier. "All right," she conceded. Richard gave her a hug, then climbed back onto the counter while she took the eggs, cheese and milk from the refrigerator.

"I was looking around your garden and noticed some of those roses you were telling me about. Where'd you find those pretty white ones?"

"Oh, this place and that," she said, and while she was pleased by his interest, the less he knew about her venture into Bitter End the better.

"You went there, didn't you?" he asked, lowering his voice.

"There?"

"Don't play games with me, Savannah. You're no good at it."

Her cheeks flushed hot pink. Richard was right, she'd never been any good at games. He was curious about the ghost town and this wasn't the first time he'd bombarded her with questions. Some about roses, others about the town itself.

"Did you go inside any of the buildings?" Richard asked. "They're still standing, right? Imagine that after all these years. What stories those walls could tell! It amazes me, you know, that Bitter End could be sleeping in those hills with only a handful of people even knowing about its existence."

"It is rather remarkable," Savannah agreed.

"I bet the buildings were in sad shape?"

"I didn't investigate the town itself," she said. The cemetery was as far as she got. Whatever was there had driven her back before she'd set foot in the actual town. But she'd know the answer to her brother's questions soon enough. Today was it, she'd decided. She was going back for a second visit, despite all Grady's efforts to keep her away.

"So where exactly is it?" Richard asked.

"Oh, sort of east of here," she said vaguely. "I had a hard time finding it." That was all she planned to say on the matter.

"Weren't you afraid?" he teased.

She wasn't sure how to describe her wariness. "Not really," she said, downplaying the eerie sensation she'd experienced on her first visit. She added the beaten eggs to the small skillet as the butter sizzled.

"I really don't think visiting the place again is a good idea," Richard surprised her by saying. Not that *she* wanted him there, but a few days ago, he'd certainly been dropping hints to that effect. He buttered the toast when it popped up and sat down at the table, awaiting his breakfast.

"I *have* to go back," she said, surprised she had to fight Richard on this, too. Grady and Laredo had formed an uneasy partnership in their efforts to keep her from returning. "There're bound to be other roses," she explained, although it wasn't necessary. All three men knew her reasons. "I might find an even rarer form. I can't tell you how thrilled I was with my original discovery."

"Think carefully before you go back," Richard said, smiling gratefully when she set the plate of steaming eggs in front of him. "You'd be wise to heed Grady's advice,

Savannah. A ghost town isn't any place for you to go exploring alone.''

"Earlier you said you wanted to come along. You—''

"I said that?'' He flattened his hand against his chest. "Not me. I'm as chicken as they come. You won't catch me anywhere close to Bitter End. I have a healthy respect for the supernatural.''

Savannah refused to be dissuaded, but she didn't intend to discuss it further. She'd do what she did the last time—steal away before anyone knew she was gone.

GRADY SAT IN HIS OFFICE and pinched the bridge of his nose, hoping that would help him focus on the long row of ledger numbers. He hadn't slept more than a couple of hours the entire night. Instead, he'd been leaning over the toilet, examining parts of it that were never meant to be viewed from this perspective.

Hard liquor had never agreed with him. Especially in quantity. After he'd embarrassed himself and Savannah, he'd holed up in his office with a bottle of cheap whiskey. The good stuff had disappeared, as he'd told his sister—but he hadn't been in any mood to appreciate the difference.

This morning his head throbbed with a vengeance. He couldn't think, couldn't work. Richard had been back less than a week, and already Grady was reduced to a useless piece of... He didn't finish the thought.

The phone pealed and he slammed his eyes closed as the sound pierced his brain, shattering what little serenity he'd managed to recover. He waited for Savannah to answer.

No one knew he was in his office, and that was the way he wanted it.

The phone rang a second time and then a third. Where

the hell was Savannah? If not her, Richard? Rather than suffer the agony of a fourth ring, Grady grabbed the receiver.

"Who the hell is it?" he snarled.

A shocked silence greeted him, followed by a sob, then tears and "Mommy, Mommy."

Damn. It'd been Maggie for Savannah, and he'd frightened the poor kid half out of her wits.

"Maggie," he shouted, wanting to apologize for his outburst. Apologize was all he seemed to do these days. He felt faint stirrings of hope when he heard someone pick up the receiver.

"Maggie, listen—"

"It's Caroline," she interrupted coolly. "And this must be Grady." She didn't give him a chance to respond before she added, "What exactly did you say to Maggie to upset her like this?"

"I didn't know. I thought…" Even his tongue refused to work properly.

"Obviously you *didn't* think."

He could hear Maggie softly weeping in the background.

"I'm sorry, Caroline," he said. "Hell, I didn't know it was Maggie. I certainly didn't mean to frighten her."

"What's gotten into you, Grady?"

He braced his forehead against his hand. If the answer was that simple, he would've saved himself a great deal of embarrassment. The truth was he didn't know any longer.

"You made an ass of yourself last night."

"Nice of you to remind me." Leave it to a woman to kick a man when he was down.

"You had too much to drink."

"You brought me one of those beers," he felt obliged to remind her.

"So this is all *my* fault?"

Grady closed his eyes at her outrage. "No," he admitted, feeling about as low as a man could get. "I accept full responsibility."

The silence stretched between them until Caroline slowly released a deep breath and asked, "Where's Savannah?"

"I don't know. I expected her to pick up the phone." Clearly so had Maggie, who continued to weep noisily in the background.

"Is she all right?" Caroline asked.

"She was this morning." And not afraid to set him down a peg or two, although he knew he'd asked for it.

Maggie's cries subsided into soft muffled sounds.

"What are you doing home?" he asked Caroline. She should be at the post office, but then, he wasn't one to talk, seeing as he should be out on the range with Wiley. Or working in the barn with Laredo Smith.

"Maggie wasn't feeling well this morning, so I took the day off."

"How's she doing?"

"She's feeling better—or she was," Caroline said pointedly.

"I'd like to talk to her if you'd let me, so I can apologize." He wasn't sure he knew *how* to talk to a five-year-old, but he didn't want her cringing in terror every time she was out at the ranch. She was a sweet little girl and Savannah was deeply attached to her.

"I don't know if she'll talk to you."

"Ask her, will you?" His hand tightened around the receiver while he waited. In the background he could hear Caroline reasoning with the child. He was somewhat amused when he heard her compare him to the beast in *Beauty and the Beast*. He made a lot of loud noises and sounded mean, Caroline said, but deep down he was really a prince who'd been put under a spell.

Caroline returned to the phone a couple of minutes later. "I'm sorry, Grady, but I can't convince her to give you a second chance."

"I can't say I blame her," Grady said with a sigh. "I was pretty rough when I answered."

"She called to tell Savannah she had a tummy ache."

"My kind of sympathy wasn't what she was looking for, was it."

The sound of Caroline's half chuckle did more to lift his spirits than anything had that day.

"I guess you could say that," she said softly.

"I have been a beast, haven't I."

"You could say that, too."

"Since she won't let me talk to her, will you tell Maggie I'm sorry? I promise I won't shout at her again." He didn't know if it would do any good, but it was the best he could manage. The next time Maggie visited the ranch, he'd try to square things with her.

"I'll let Savannah know you phoned," he said, reaching for a pen. If he didn't write it down, he'd forget, and he didn't think Caroline would be willing to forgive him that on top of everything else.

They exchanged goodbyes and he replaced the receiver.

With an effort he glanced down at the ledger and reached for the calculator, determined to make good use of his time. He couldn't laze in bed until noon like his worthless brother.

LAREDO ASSUMED he'd find Savannah in the rose garden, but she was nowhere in sight. Nor was she in the house.

He'd done everything short of knocking on her bedroom door.

Grady had disappeared, as well, but that was more a blessing than a matter of concern.

Unsure where to search next, Laredo headed back to the barn. It was one of the last places he expected to find Savannah. A niggling sense of fear refused to leave him. She'd looked pale that morning, and although he hadn't been eager to clash with Grady so soon after their last confrontation, he wasn't about to let him harass Savannah.

The barn door creaked as he pushed it open. Light spilled into the interior and Savannah spun around. Her eyes instantly widened with guilt.

Laredo had no idea what she'd been doing, but clearly it was something she didn't want anyone knowing.

"Savannah?"

"Hi." Her smile was a bit sheepish.

"What are you doing in here?"

"Nothing. I was—"

"Savannah," he said, and held out his arms, needing to reassure her. She didn't hesitate, not so much as a second. He brought her into his embrace and hugged her. "Don't ever play poker, sweetheart. Your expression's a dead giveaway."

Her arms circled his waist and she pressed her face to his shoulder. "I'm so sorry about what happened last night," she said.

This was the first chance they'd had to discuss the incident, but Laredo preferred to drop the entire thing. He'd been at fault, too, eager to put her brother in his place for embarrassing Savannah. And he'd been angry after his chat with Hennessey, knowing Grady had instigated the sheriff's questioning.

"Let's put it behind us, okay?"

He felt her deep sigh. "Is that what you want?" she asked in a solemn voice.

"Yeah."

"I'm willing to forget it—except for one thing." She tilted her head back and gazed at him with wide adoring eyes.

"What's that?" Laredo didn't know what he'd done to deserve having such a beautiful woman look at him that way.

"I could put the…incident behind me if Grady hadn't cheated me out of my sweetheart dance."

"Not all of it."

"I begrudge every second he stole from me."

Laredo kissed the top of her head and reached behind him to take hold of her hands. "Don't you hear the music?" he asked.

"Music?" Her eyes narrowed as if she was straining to hear before she realized what he was doing. She smiled then, and it was all he could do not to cover her mouth with his.

"I believe there *is* music in here," she said, her face alight with happiness.

"There must be."

Laredo danced her about the barn floor, making turns so wide that her skirt flared straight out as they whirled around. Savannah threw back her head and laughed with such pure joy Laredo was soon smiling himself.

They whirled faster and faster until they were both winded and ready to collapse with laughter. Savannah pressed her hand to her throat as she drew in a deep breath.

"Okay, confess," he said once he'd caught his own breath. He leaned against the wall and watched as the amusement left her.

"Confess?"

"What were you up to earlier?"

He watched as she shifted her feet a couple of times before she lowered her head. "You'll be angry with me."

Laredo didn't think that was possible. "Why?"

"I was about to break the promise I made you. I—I'm sorry...."

Then it dawned on him. She'd been gathering equipment to sneak away to that damned ghost town. He exhaled sharply, grateful he'd found her when he had. He was disappointed, too. He'd expected Savannah to be a woman of her word.

"I'm sorry," she said again, with such genuine regret that he couldn't help forgiving her. "Richard and I were talking about Bitter End this morning, and I felt this urge to go there again. Now. Today. I have to, Laredo. Because of the roses." She glanced down at her feet. "And I didn't want Richard to know. Or Grady. I wasn't sure where you were...and I've got to leave quickly." She raised her head to look at him. "Can you come with me?" she asked, her expressive eyes filled with hope. "It won't take much time. I'll leave Grady a note and explain."

Grady might owe him a favor, but Laredo didn't feel ready to collect it quite this soon. Then he changed his mind.

"All right," he said, "we'll do it."

She clapped her hands, then forgetting herself, leaped forward and kissed him on the mouth. "I'll pack up a lunch and afterward we can have a picnic."

He hadn't the heart to disappoint her, but his idea of

how he wanted to spend the day wasn't sitting in some field full of bluebonnets, lingering over sandwiches. Not even with Savannah... He thought of all the chores that awaited him. Chores Grady counted on him to do.

"How long will we be?"

"Not too long," she promised. "All I want to do is walk around and see if there are any other roses. We won't stay."

He nodded.

"There's a lovely spot a few miles down the road where the river bends. We can have lunch there." She wasn't about to drop this picnic idea of hers, and really, he supposed, it was a small thing to ask.

With their plans set, Laredo loaded the shovels and other tools into the back of the pickup. As he did, an uneasiness settled over him. Apparently what Grady had told him about the place had made a stronger impact than he'd realized. His uneasiness grew into dread and refused to leave him.

They weren't even off the ranch yet, and already he was convinced they shouldn't go.

Chapter Eight

The truck pitched and heaved, first left and then right, as they neared Bitter End. Savannah hung on as best she could but her shoulders continued to slam against Laredo's, jarring them both. Thankfully they were able to follow the tire tracks from her last visit, otherwise she wasn't sure she could have located it a second time.

"I can't believe you found this place on your own," Laredo said, his hands gripping the steering wheel tightly.

"It wasn't easy—took me weeks of searching."

More than once she'd been tempted to forsake the idea, but the thought of finding old roses had spurred her onward. Her patience had been richly rewarded. Not only had she discovered the White Lady Banks, her most valuable find to date, but on that same day she'd come across Laredo.

The truck pitched sharply and Laredo cursed under his breath.

"We're pretty close now," she assured him. His face was tense with concentration, and although he drove cautiously, he couldn't avoid jolting the truck on the rough ground. There was barely even a track.

Savannah was grateful Laredo had agreed to escort her back to the ghost town, but what she looked forward to even more was their picnic. They were rarely alone. This stolen time was bound to be special.

Laredo eased the truck to a stop when they could go no farther.

"It's only a short walk from here," she promised.

The trek was difficult, through brush and dense cedars, and they were both breathless before the town came into view.

"So this is Bitter. End," Laredo muttered as he climbed over rocks to a limestone ledge that overlooked the town. He offered Savannah his hand.

She took it and stepped up. From the outskirts Bitter End resembled any other ghost town. A row of forsaken buildings lined the main street, four or five on each side, in various states of disrepair, various stages of dying. Paintless shutters hung crookedly by empty windows. The stillness and lack of sound gave it an eerie unreal feeling. Wind-tossed tumbleweeds had wedged in the corners and along the boardwalk. A quick inspection didn't reveal any visible plant life, but there had to be some roses. The ones in the cemetery had survived. Others would've, too.

The largest building in town was the church, which sat on a hill at the far end of town, next to the cemetery. Time had left it remarkably untouched. It'd remained white and unblemished except for the charred steeple, which had apparently been struck by lightning. At the other end of town was a corral.

They clambered down a rocky embankment into the town itself. Then it happened just as it had on her first visit. The feeling of sadness and pain. Whatever possessed Bitter End wasn't ghosts or spirits, of that she was fairly certain, but a sorrow so strong even the years hadn't dimmed it.

She looked at Laredo, who faced the town squarely, feet slightly apart, ready, it seemed, for anything. He stood there silently, as if he was listening and yet heard nothing.

"Do you feel it?" she whispered. Normal tones didn't seem right. On her previous visit she hadn't murmured a word. She'd been in and out of the town within ten minutes. Just long enough to dig up the roses and replace them with a bush from her own garden.

"Are you sure you want to go ahead with this?" Laredo asked. He, too, spoke in a whisper, unwilling to disturb whatever it was that awaited them.

Savannah slipped her arm through his. "I'm positive."

"Then let's get it over with and get the hell out."

"There aren't any ghosts here," she told him, still in a whisper.

"Whatever you say." He smiled for the first time since their arrival.

"It won't take long to look for more roses," she said. The presence of another person—someone she trusted—made the town seem a little less frightening.

If Laredo wasn't in such an all-fired hurry to leave, it might have been fun to explore the interior of some of the buildings. But then again, Savannah had the distinct impression they were trespassing as it was.

"Where do you want to start?" Laredo asked as they neared the main street.

"Anyplace is fine. I was in the cemetery earlier." She motioned toward the church and the graveyard behind it. They walked side by side, holding hands. His warm grasp lent her reassurance.

The farther they went into town, the stronger the sense of sorrow became. With each step down the narrow street, the feeling grew darker. During her last visit she'd hurried through Bitter End as quickly as possible on her way to the cemetery, trying to shake off the sense of misery and unease.

She'd actually enjoyed visiting the graveyard. The sensation hadn't been nearly as powerful there, and she'd been fascinated by the headstones. Most of the names and dates on the simple markers were no longer legible, but that hadn't stopped her from picturing the kind of life the people of Bitter End had lived. It would have been a harsh existence, battling hunger, disease and the elements.

Savannah recalled the stories she'd read about the frontier days when Texas had been wild and unforgiving. Stories she would one day read to her own children.

Her own children.

The thought caught her unprepared. All these years Savannah had assumed she'd never marry. Since meeting Laredo she'd begun to believe that all things were possible for her. A husband and a family of her own. Despite the eeriness of the place, Savannah's heart gladdened.

After a few minutes exploring the town's streets, Savannah realized that the trip had been a waste of time and energy. Whatever flowers, roses or otherwise, once bloomed in Bitter End had long since died. Nothing grew inside the town. Nothing. Everything was dead, including the land itself.

The lone tree, an oak with gnarled limbs, was hollow and lifeless. It stood in silent testimony to a time and place long forgotten.

"Don't you think it's a bit bizarre that there's nothing alive here? Not even a weed?" Laredo commented.

She nodded. The only plants that had survived one-hundred-plus years were the roses she'd discovered at the cemetery. "I want to go back," she said.

"I couldn't agree with you more," Laredo murmured.

"I mean, to the cemetery," she said.

He hesitated. "Are you sure that's wise?"

"I don't know, but I'm curious about the grave site where I found the roses." It didn't add up in Savannah's mind. If those roses had survived, then it made sense that other plants would have, too.

"In my humble opinion," Laredo said, his words barely audible, "we shouldn't tempt fate. Let's leave while the leaving's good. All right?"

His hand gripped Savannah's with such force that her fingers throbbed. He wasn't intentionally hurting her, she knew, but reacting to the tension inside him.

"All right," she agreed. "We'll go. I'll look some other time."

"No." The force behind the single word brought her up short.

"I don't want you coming back here," he said with an urgency that baffled her. "Not for anything. Understand? This place gives me the creeps."

Despite her love for him, she couldn't make that kind of promise. "No. Someday there might be a very good reason for me to return."

Clearly, he wanted to argue the point, but right then, leaving appeared to be a higher priority. Frequently looking over his shoulder, Laredo led her back toward the faint path that would take them to the truck.

As they walked, the sensation gradually lifted from her shoulders. Savannah could feel it slipping away. Like a silk scarf dragged across a palm, the sensation faded until it was completely gone.

Once they reached the pickup, Laredo helped Savannah inside, then climbed in himself. He couldn't seem to start the engine fast enough. His anxiety, even greater than her own, was contagious.

Savannah didn't want to know what had created the feeling that pervaded Bitter End. There was nothing good in that town and maybe there never had been.

LIFE WAS FILLED with mysteries, Laredo told himself. The answers weren't always meant to be known. That was the way he felt about this ghost town. Grady hadn't said much about it, only that it wasn't a safe place for Savannah. Her brother couldn't trust her not to return on her own, so he'd put aside his dislike and distrust of Laredo and sought his help.

For the first time Laredo appreciated Grady's fears. He didn't know what the hell had happened in that town. But he didn't need to know. As far as he was concerned, Bitter End could continue as it had for more than a hundred years without interruption from him.

He leaned against the tree trunk and watched Savannah unpack the picnic basket. He still wasn't keen on lazing away the afternoon under a flowering pecan, but his objection to the wasted time felt much less urgent now.

The spot she'd chosen for their picnic was as lovely as she'd promised. The river flowed swiftly nearby, the clean sound of water a sharp contrast to what he'd experienced a short time before.

Savannah finished unloading the wicker basket and quickly assembled them each a plate—roast-beef sandwiches, yesterday's potato salad, homemade pickles. They ate in companionable silence for a while, then both spoke at once.

"You felt it, too, didn't you?" she asked.

"Was it the same as before?" he asked.

They paused and grinned, then Laredo took the lead.

"I'll tell you what," he said. "Let's not talk about the town."

"Why not?"

He wasn't sure if she was disappointed or relieved. "I want to talk about you."

"Me?" She shook her head. "You already know everything."

"No, I'm sure I don't. For instance, who taught you to cook like this?" He couldn't remember a time he'd eaten better. Not in years. Not since he was a child, when he'd been too young to appreciate a home-cooked meal.

"My mother loved cooking. Baking, too. Mealtime was a matter of pride to her. I guess we're more alike than I realized." Her eyes grew wide. "You would have liked her, Laredo—she was a wonderful woman."

He didn't doubt that, not with the way he felt about Savannah. Relaxed as he was, the sun behind him, the sound of the river singing nearby, Laredo yawned, lulled by the serenity of the spot. "You'd like my mother, too."

He hadn't meant to talk about himself, but once he'd mentioned his mother, she wouldn't let the subject drop. Before long he was answering her questions, talking about his mother in Tulsa. About her being widowed in 1972. And how she'd moved back to the same house where she'd been born and raised, the house where she still lived. How she'd been dating the same man for twenty years without any plan to marry him.

"I know I'd like her," Savannah said wistfully. Then she lowered her gaze until her long lashes grazed the high arch of her cheek. "Would you... Never mind." Savannah reached for a blade of grass and nervously twisted it around her finger.

"Would I what?" he prodded, enjoying her discomfort. Little did she realize that he'd do just about anything for her. All she had to do was ask.

Her eyes fleetingly held his before she glanced away. "Would you like to put your head in my lap?" she asked.

This was what dreams were made of, he decided as he rested his neck against her thigh. It didn't take long for her fingers to weave their way into his hair, her touch soft and gentle. A memory rushed forward, one of his father and mother. His mother cutting his father's hair in the kitchen. Laredo couldn't have been more than four at the time, but he recalled the loving way his mother's hands had smoothed back the hair from his father's brow. His father had reached for her hand and kissed her palm.

Without realizing it, Laredo caught Savannah's fingers and brought them to his lips. His heart constricted with the strength of emotion that coursed through him.

He didn't intend to kiss her, but that was a natural progression. As natural as drawing his next breath. He lifted his head from the sanctuary of her lap and gently met her mouth with his. The hunger that surged to fire in his blood stunned him. The strength of his desire would have frightened her had he acted on it, Laredo thought. Instead, he involved himself in the kiss, his lips lingering on hers.

One kiss, he promised himself. But it soon became obvious that a single kiss wasn't enough for either of them. They exchanged one after another, each more intense than the last. Laredo had to call on every ounce of willpower he possessed to stop.

"I like it when you kiss me," Savannah whispered. She kept her eyes closed as she spoke.

"I like it, too," he confessed.

"Don't stop," she pleaded.

Once again Laredo found himself in the position of being unable to refuse her.

The kiss was even better than the others; he'd assumed that was impossible. Savannah lay on the blanket, smiling up at him and he leaned over her.

"You taste so good I don't want you to ever stop," she whispered when he hesitated.

"Sweetheart, you don't know what you're asking."

"I do," she murmured, her mouth moist and slightly swollen from his kisses. "I want you to kiss me forever."

That didn't sound like a bad plan to Laredo, but sooner or later, kissing wouldn't be enough to satisfy either one of them. They were fast approaching that point now.

"Savannah," he whispered, wondering how he could explain why it wasn't a good idea to continue.

He didn't get a chance. She locked her arms around his neck and drew his mouth down to hers again. He tried to show her without words what she did to him. This kiss was fierce, as fierce as his growing need.

He urged her lips apart and swept her mouth with his tongue, fully expecting— Hell, he didn't know *what* he was expecting. Certainly not this acceptance, this welcoming. His breath jammed in his lungs as the kiss deepened. While he waged war with his needs, she returned his lovemaking with an eagerness that destroyed his restraint. Her nails dug into his shoulders as if to bring him closer, become part of him. Laredo was convinced she didn't really grasp the overwhelming physical intensity of his reaction, didn't realize what she was doing to him.

Above all, he didn't want her ending up in a sexual situation she wasn't ready for.

When he could endure no more, he abruptly broke off the kiss and rolled away. His shoulders heaved with the strength of will it had taken to leave her.

"Did I do something wrong?" she asked after a moment.

He waited until he'd caught his breath before he answered. "I wouldn't say that."

"Then why did you stop?"

He closed his eyes. "I don't think you understand—"

"Don't treat me like a child, Laredo. I know exactly what was happening."

He felt depleted; he hadn't the energy to argue with her. She made him vulnerable. Much more of this kissing would have sent him over the edge. He knew his limits and they'd been reached.

He sat up and smiled. Or at least made the effort to smile. In an attempt to clear his head, he took several deep breaths.

"I called about the repairs to the truck," he said, not looking at her. He focused on the tree limbs overhead, hoping she realized why he'd abruptly changed the subject.

His announcement was greeted with silence.

"Paul said the parts were in and all he needed was the go-ahead from me." Laredo paused and waited for a response.

More silence.

Finally she said, "I know what you're doing, Laredo."

"Do you?" He doubted it.

"You're telling me that you're leaving Promise as soon as you can."

So she did know, and if she was that smart, she'd probably figure out the rest. "I don't want to hurt you, Savannah."

"You couldn't," she said, her voice small. "You've already brought me such incredible happiness. When you do...leave—" she appeared to have trouble saying the word "—don't worry that I'll do anything to stop you. I'm grateful for each day we can be together. Grateful for each moment...each kiss."

He didn't see it that way. After all, he was the one in *her* debt. "I think we should get back before anyone misses us." He was strongly tempted to resume their lovemaking, and he couldn't be sure he possessed the determination to resist.

"Not yet," she pleaded softly. "I left a note in the kitchen so no one'll worry."

He didn't know what would happen if they kissed again—and didn't think he could afford to find out. He stood, removing himself from temptation.

"Just a few more moments." She regarded him with such longing he found it impossible to refuse her.

"All right," he said, and sat back down on the blanket. "But only a few minutes longer. Okay? And no kissing."

She nodded and thanked him with the sweetest of smiles.

A few minutes soon became two hours. Savannah closed her eyes and was immediately asleep. Laredo wondered if she'd gotten much rest the night before. He knew *he* hadn't. He suspected that the only one who'd enjoyed the luxury of a night's uninterrupted sleep was Richard.

He knew how Savannah felt about her brother and feared it was only a matter of time before Richard disappointed her. Laredo didn't want to see that happen, but he was helpless to protect her.

Uncomfortable with his thoughts, Laredo sat against the tree and watched Savannah, appreciating her gentle beauty. Each minute was a gift; she'd been the one to express that thought, and he, too, had discovered the truth of it.

The world, his mother once told him, had a way of making all things equal. A divine order. *We receive back what we give,* or something along those lines. He hadn't paid close attention at the time and now wished he had. But it seemed to him that meeting Savannah made up for everything that had ever gone wrong in his life. Every broken promise. Every unmet expectation, every unfair act.

But why did he have to meet her *now?* He snapped off a blade of grass and chewed on the end. Why would he meet this woman—and fall in love with her—when he had nothing to offer but hardship?

Laredo loved Savannah; he'd admitted that early on. He loved her enough to leave her, rather than ask her to scrimp and sacrifice with him. She deserved far better. He refused to cheat her of the comfort and certitude that were her right.

ELLIE FRASIER was busy in the back room dealing with a shipment from one of her main suppliers when Richard Weston strolled in. He wore a crisp pair of jeans, his fancy boots and brand-new Stetson, and looked more like a country singer than a rancher.

"So this is where you've been hiding yourself," he said. He gazed at her boldly, eyes roaming from her hair to her booted feet, letting her know without words that he liked what he saw. Ellie wasn't opposed to a bit of flattery now and again. Lord knew Glen and the other men in her life were damned stingy with their appreciation.

It had come as a shock to see Richard again after all these years. At first she hadn't recognized him. As a schoolgirl she'd had a crush on him. Richard Weston had been an "older" man, both handsome and charming. That much hadn't changed.

"I thought I'd let you take me to lunch," he said, glancing over her shoulder to read the clipboard.

"I don't have time today." She wouldn't have minded spending her lunch break with him, but she was simply too busy. She'd taken on her father's responsibilities, as well as handling her own. Glen had suggested she hire someone to look after the books, and while she knew he was right, she'd delayed.

"You could use some time off," Richard said, evidently disappointed she'd refused him. "And I'd love the company."

"I wish I could."

"Come on," he said. "It'll do you good." He sent her an appealing boyish grin. "I can be a fun guy, you know."

"I noticed." Ellie didn't bother to disguise her smile. The welcome-home party had been just the tonic her sinking spirits needed. The pressures of holding down the feed store and the worries over her father's health had exhausted her.

Glen stopped off a couple of times a week to offer moral support. He was her best friend, and his down-to-earth humor had gone a long way to bolster her courage and resolve. At Richard's party she'd relaxed and enjoyed herself for the first time in weeks. She'd danced with Glen and with Richard—and Richard had even kissed her. It was the closest thing to a date she'd had in months.

"Maybe I will escape for an hour or so," she said, surprising herself. "The world won't come to an end without me."

"Great." A smile lit up his handsome face.

Not too often was a woman given the opportunity to realize her schoolgirl dreams, Ellie mused. Okay, so she'd been fifteen and impressionable, but Richard Weston had been by far the most attractive boy in Promise. There hadn't been a girl in school who wouldn't have given...whatever for the chance to go out with him. Richard had played it cool, though. He'd never dated one girl for any length of time. In that sense he hadn't changed; he must be close to thirty now and had yet to settle down.

"Where do you want to go?" he asked.

Seeing as there were very few restaurants in town, Ellie didn't figure there were many options. "You choose."

"How about your house?" He leaned close enough for her to catch a whiff of his musk-scented aftershave.

"My house?"

"Sure, we can rustle up something for lunch and then snuggle on the sofa for a while and talk about old times."

He had a smile that would charm a snake. "What old times?" Ellie asked.

"We can make that part up as we go along." His voice fell, heavy with suggestion.

"Richard!" The man was a blatant flirt.

"Why not?"

"First, I'm the world's worst cook. Trust me, you wouldn't want to eat anything I've made myself. Second, snuggling up on the sofa, tempting as it sounds, is the last thing I have time for."

"I bet I could convince you otherwise."

"Really?" This guy was too much. She shook her head and tossed the clipboard on a shelf facedown. "And just how do you intend to do that?"

He grinned that boyish grin again and reached for her hand, tugging her after him.

"Hey, where are we going?"

"Someplace private—where I can show you what I mean." He looked furtively around, then pulled her inside the office and closed the door.

"Richard?"

The next thing she knew he had her pinned against the wall. He'd kissed her at the party; she'd enjoyed the attention—and the kiss hadn't been bad, either. Maybe it was just what she'd needed to revive her energy and enthusiasm. All work and no play had dulled her senses, but Richard Weston had brought them back to life.

His kiss now was deep and sultry. By the time he lifted his head from hers, Ellie's knees felt weak.

"How was that?" he asked.

"Not bad." Her reply was breathless, despite her effort to sound casual. Her hands were flattened against the wall behind her, as if to prop her up. She took a deep breath. Her emotions must be in a sorry state, indeed. In fact, everything in her life seemed to be in a constant state of upheaval.

"There's a lot more where that came from," he promised. He ran the tip of his index finger down the V of her shirt, trailing it lower, close to the curve of her breast.

"Unfortunately," she said, slapping his hand away, "I can't squeeze an affair into my busy schedule."

"Where there's a will there's a way."

"Richard, please, I'm flattered but—"

He interrupted her with a second kiss. This one wet and seductive and a little too rough.

Ellie couldn't believe she was allowing this to continue. What she'd said was true—she was flattered, but she wasn't one to indulge in casual sex. Or casual anything.

"I've got responsibilities."

"Don't we all?"

"Richard!"

"That's my name and I certainly like to hear you say it, but not quite like that." His hands massaged her tired shoulders. Against every dictate of her will, Ellie closed her eyes.

"I want you to whisper my name when we're in bed…"

She gasped. "I can't believe you're actually serious!"

"I've never been more serious. I thought about you when I was away…and I wondered if you were married. I'm glad you're not."

"You didn't even know who I was!"

"Are you kidding? Believe me, I knew, but a guy can get arrested for thinking the way I did about you back then."

Ellie recognized a lie when she heard one. "I appreciate the offer, I truly do, and if I have a vacancy anytime soon, I'll give you a call."

"Hey, don't be hasty here. We were going to lunch, remember?"

A loud knock sounded on the office door. "Ellie, are you in there?"

Glen Patterson. Arriving like the cavalry the minute she needed rescuing. His timing couldn't have been better.

"Come on in," she called, moving toward the door.

Glen let himself inside and frowned when he saw Richard.

"I was trying to talk Ellie into getting away for an hour or so. To have lunch," Richard explained, his smile as friendly as if they'd been involved in harmless conversation instead of a kiss.

It might have helped if Glen had displayed a shred of

jealousy, but he didn't. "Good idea," he said, glancing at Ellie. "You need to get out more."

"I can't today. Maybe some other time," she said, and scampered past the two men.

Ten minutes later Glen found her in the storeroom going through the order. "Richard's gone?" she asked.

"Yeah. He hasn't changed much, has he?"

"How do you mean?"

Glen didn't answer until she glanced up from the clipboard.

"He's a wheeler-dealer."

"So I noticed," she said with a chuckle. She fanned her face and deliberately expelled a breath.

"Hey, what does that mean?"

"What do you *think* it means?"

Glen thought about that for a moment, and either didn't get it or wasn't willing to say it out loud.

"Let's put it like this," Ellie said. "Richard Weston was interested in a whole lot more than lunch."

Glen's eyes widened considerably.

"Why does that shock you? Does it surprise you to realize other men might look on me as more than one of the guys?"

Again he took his time responding. "Not really. You're about the best damn friend I've ever had. And you're game for just about anything."

"Within limits," she said, thinking of Richard's proposal.

"Within limits," Glen agreed, then laughed. "Hell, maybe it isn't such a bad idea, after all."

"You and me?"

He looked stunned. "Hell, no. You and Richard."

Chapter Nine

Sunday morning Maggie slipped into Savannah's pew and leaned against her just as Wade McMillen approached the pulpit. Slipping an arm around the child, Savannah pulled her close, acknowledging just how much she'd come to love her friend's daughter. They'd formed a special bond, and it wasn't unusual for Maggie to sit with Savannah during church services.

A talented speaker, Wade often used humor in his sermons. The theme of this morning's talk revolved around the opportunities God presented. Savannah found herself laughing along with the rest of the congregation as Wade relayed the story of a man stuck on a rooftop in a flash flood.

Three times a rescue team had come for him, and each time the man insisted that God would provide. The man died and went to heaven and confronted the Lord, demanding to know why his faith had gone unanswered.

"I sent the Red Cross, a boat and a helicopter," God told him. "What more could I have done?"

Wade had a way of communicating truth without being obtrusive, dogmatic or self-righteous. Savannah often wondered why he remained unmarried when any number of eligible young women in Promise would have been thrilled to be his wife. It was a frequent source of interest, gossip and speculation at any gathering of church members.

Maggie squirmed as the sermon drew to a close. She smiled up at Savannah and silently turned the pages of her hymnal, waiting until the choir stood to sing and she could see her mother.

The love she felt for this child poured through Savannah's heart, and with it a desire so deep and so long denied that it bordered on pain. Until she'd met Laredo, she'd relinquished the dream of ever becoming a bride—and, of course, along with that, a mother.

The yearning to bear a child of her own burned in her heart now. She closed her eyes and her mind instantly filled with the image of a young boy of five or six. He was dressed in jeans, a shirt, hat and boots, a miniature version of Laredo. The child trailed after him as they headed toward the corral. Father and son. Their child, hers and Laredo's. The thought moved her so strongly, she battled back a sudden urge to weep. Savannah felt a thrill of pure happiness at the sheer wonder of having found Laredo.

What a wonderful husband and father he'd be. Laredo had been patient and gentle with Maggie from the first, while Grady groped clumsily in his effort to make friends with the little girl. Laredo was a natural with children, and it was easy to imagine him surrounded by a whole brood of them.

Most important of all Laredo loved her. She was confident of that. Not that he openly confessed his feelings. But Savannah didn't need a formal declaration or flowery words to know how he felt. A hundred times, more, he'd shown her his feelings.

Laredo was protective of her, his manner traditional in

the very best way. He was thoughtful and considerate, sensitive to her moods and needs. As far as Savannah was concerned, his actions spoke far more eloquently than anything he could ever say. Last week, for instance, while she was working on the design for her catalog, he'd brought in a cup of coffee, set it on the desk beside her, kissed her cheek and silently left the room. Another day he'd seen her carrying a heavy load of laundry outside to hang on the clothesline, and he'd rushed to her side and carried it for her.

Wiley had teased Laredo unmercifully that day, pretending he was in dire need of assistance, mincing around and flapping his hands in a ridiculous imitation of a woman in distress. Laredo had paid no attention to his antics.

After the Sunday service was dismissed, Caroline met Savannah in the front of the church. "I thought you said Richard was coming with you this morning," her friend said.

"I thought he would." Savannah was deeply disappointed in her younger brother. Grady was barely speaking to her, which was nothing new, and all because she continued to champion her brother's cause. Despite Richard's reprehensible actions, he *was* their brother. No matter what he'd done, she wouldn't allow Grady to throw him off the ranch. He had nowhere else to go. He'd told her he was still waiting for the money that was supposed to be in the mail; he seemed so sure it would be arriving any day. Because she believed him—*had* to believe him—she'd lent him money herself, although she didn't let Grady or Laredo know that.

"Do you think he's ever going to change?" Caroline asked. "I'm just so afraid that if you trust him, you might be setting yourself up for heartache."

"He's my brother," Savannah said simply. She was convinced that their mother, had she been alive, wouldn't have allowed Grady to kick Richard out, either.

"There's something different about you," Caroline said when she reached her car.

"Different?" Although she formed the word as a question, Savannah knew what Caroline meant. And it was true. She wasn't the same woman she'd been as little as a month ago. "I'm happy," she said, blushing profusely. "Really truly happy."

"Laredo?" Caroline asked.

Savannah lowered her eyes and nodded.

"I like Laredo," Maggie announced. "And Richard."

"What about Grady?" Caroline coaxed her daughter.

Maggie pinched her lips together tightly. "Grady's... okay, I guess, but he yells too much."

"I don't think she's forgiven him for shouting at her over the phone. I've tried to explain that he's—"

"A beast like from *Beauty and the Beast*," Maggie supplied. "I don't care if he *is* a handsome prince. When he yells I have to cover my ears."

"Oh, Maggie," Savannah whispered, feeling wretched. "Grady likes you very much and wants to be your friend, too."

"Then he shouldn't shout at me on the phone," she said in an eminently reasonable tone.

Savannah wanted to shake Grady. She didn't know what had possessed him to explode at Maggie. His only excuse, weak as it was, had something to do with not knowing who was on the other end of the line.

It was getting to the point that she barely knew what to think of her own brother. She wasn't sure who'd changed the most in the past few weeks, Grady or her. She knew having Richard around troubled him, and while

Grady talked about throwing Richard out, she sensed that he struggled with what was right the same way she did. Richard was a charmer, but of the two men, Grady was the one with heart.

"Would you like to join us for dinner?" Savannah asked her friends, thinking it might help Maggie feel more comfortable with Grady. "I've got a huge roast in the oven, and fresh-strawberry shortcake."

"Mmm." Maggie licked her lips. "Strawberries are my favorite." Wide-eyed, she looked up at her mother.

"Not today, Savannah. I'll take a rain check."

"But Mommy..."

Maggie's disappointment was a soothing balm to Savannah's own. Since the phone incident Caroline hadn't been out to the ranch. Whenever Savannah suggested she visit, her friend came up with a convenient excuse, or in this instance, just a polite refusal. It bothered Savannah and she hoped the uneasiness between Grady and Maggie would soon resolve itself.

When Savannah arrived back at the ranch, she discovered Richard sitting on the porch, strumming his guitar and singing softly. He stopped and waved when she pulled into the yard, then strolled over to the truck.

"Where were you all morning?" he asked as if her disappearance had worried him.

"Church. I thought you said you were coming with me."

"I would've if you'd woken me up."

"You're an adult, Richard."

His fingers stilled, the pick poised above the guitar strings. "You're not angry with me, are you?"

She sighed. "No."

He grinned boyishly and continued his song while Savannah went into the house. She set her Bible aside and checked the oven. The noonday meal was the primary one on Sundays. In the evening they all fended for themselves, giving Savannah time to pursue her own interests.

An hour later Savannah served the roast, and dished up hot-from-the-oven buttermilk biscuits, mashed potatoes and gravy, corn, a large green salad and strawberry shortcake for dessert. The meal vanished in minutes with lavish compliments from Richard and quiet appreciation from Laredo, Wiley and Grady.

Everyone disappeared afterward, leaving Savannah to herself. The afternoon was lovely, the sky blue and bright, the sun warm without the intense heat of summer. Spring was Savannah's favorite time of year. After spending an hour in her garden, she arranged a vase of roses and set them in the kitchen, allowing their fragrance to fill the room.

When she'd finished, she picked up her knitting and sat on the porch, Rocket stretched out beside her. There was silence all around her, except for the soughing of wind in the greening trees and the occasional distant sound of traffic from the highway. Without informing anyone of his plans, Richard had disappeared. Grady had vanished into his office to catch up on some reading and Wiley was visiting his widow friend in Brewster. She didn't know where Laredo had gone, but she hoped he'd join her, as he often did.

Enjoying the Sunday-afternoon tranquility, Savannah lazily worked the yarn and needles. It didn't take long for Wade McMillen's message to make its way into her thoughts. *God-given opportunities.* She mulled over the opportunities that had recently come her way. Quickly, inevitably, Laredo sprang to her mind.

Deeply absorbed in her thoughts, she wasn't aware of his approach until he stepped onto the porch.

"It's a lovely afternoon, isn't it?" she said, delighted when he claimed the empty rocker beside hers. For as long as she could remember, her parents had sat in these very chairs, side by side, lifelong companions, lovers and friends.

Laredo watched her hands moving the needles and the yarn. "My mother knits, too," he said.

"My grandmother was the one who taught me." She reached for the pattern book and showed him the cardigan she was making for Maggie. The needles clicked gently as she returned to her task.

"Church this morning was great," she went on. "I enjoy Wade's sermons." She told him about the man in the flood, and Laredo laughed at the punch line, just as she knew he would. Someday she hoped Laredo would attend services with her, but she hadn't had the courage to ask him. Not yet.

Courage. She'd missed opportunity after opportunity in her life because she was afraid. Afraid of what, exactly, she didn't know. No more, she decided then and there.

"Wade got me to thinking," she said. If she didn't tell Laredo what was in her heart now, she'd always regret letting this opportunity slip by. She used her knitting as an excuse to avoid eye contact.

"Thinking?"

"About the opportunities that have come into my life...lately."

Laredo leaned back in the rocker and relaxed, closing his eyes.

"I've never dated much," she said. "I suppose it shows, doesn't it?"

He lifted his hat brim enough to look at her. "It's not a disadvantage, if that's what you're asking."

She *felt* at a disadvantage, though, talking to him about such things, but forged ahead anyway. "It's a bit of a detriment," she said, trying to disguise the trembling in her voice. Her heart beat so fast she felt nearly breathless.

"I wouldn't want to change anything about you, Savannah."

"Thank you," she whispered, encouraged by his response.

He apparently thought their conversation was over, because he sat back in the chair once more, stretched out his legs and lowered the brim of his hat.

"There's something I need to say and I'm not sure how to go about it." Her fingers felt clammy and stiff, and she let the knitting lie idle in her lap as she composed her thoughts.

"You can tell me anything, you know that."

Despite the turbulent pounding of her heart, Savannah felt a sense of calm. "Since I don't have much experience in this kind of situation, I hope you'll forgive me for speaking frankly."

She had his attention now, and he lifted the brim of his Stetson with one finger. "Situation?"

Gripping the knitting needles tightly, she continued, "I need to know if there's a proper way for a lady to speak of certain…matters with a gentleman. Matters of the heart," she added nervously.

Laredo's position didn't alter, but she thought she saw him stiffen. "That part I wouldn't know."

"I see." Her mouth grew dry with anxiety.

An awkward silence followed while she carefully weighed her words. "Considering that you seem to be as much at a loss as I am, perhaps the best way to discuss this would be in a straightforward manner. My mother used to say, 'Nothing works better than the truth.'"

"Savannah..."

He tried to stop her, but she wouldn't let him, not while she had the courage to go on. Inhaling deeply, she began to speak. "I love you, Laredo. My heart's so full, some days I don't think I can contain all this joy. I want to thank you, to let you know how grateful I am to have met you."

Her words appeared to stun him. Slowly Laredo sat upright and stared straight ahead, not responding to her words at all. If they'd brought him any pleasure, he wasn't letting it show.

She waited, her hands trembling now at the bold thing she'd said. "Perhaps I've spoken out of turn, but it seems that when a woman loves a man she—"

"Savannah," he interrupted quietly. "Don't say any more. Please."

The color of acute embarrassment erupted in her cheeks. "Is saying I love you improper?"

"There's nothing improper about you. It's me."

"You?" She was utterly confused, completely on edge. She feared what would happen next.

"I'm not the right man for you."

The relief was so great she nearly laughed aloud. "Oh, Laredo, how can you say such a thing? Nobody's ever been more right for me in my entire life."

"Savannah, I have nothing..."

"Do you think that matters?"

"Yes," he said quietly. Intensely. "It does."

She waited a moment, then told him with gentle insistence, "For most of my life my parents and then Grady were sure they knew what was right for me. The amazing part of all this is that no one ever bothered to ask my opinion. I'm thirty-one years old, and believe it or not, I know what I want. I want you. I love you."

He leaned forward and pressed his elbows to his knees as though her words had brought him pain, instead of joy.

Her back went rigid. "I apologize if I've embarrassed you."

"It's not that. Savannah, listen to me. I'm truly honored that you love me, but it won't work. It just won't work." His voice sagged with regret, with defeat.

"Is it— Don't you care for me?" It seemed impossible he didn't share her feelings. She'd been so sure. And she'd hoped that revealing *her* love would free him to acknowledge his.

He hesitated. "I..."

"If you tell me you don't return my affection, then I'll apologize and never mention it again." Although she made the offer, Savannah had no doubts. Laredo couldn't have held her or kissed her with such gentle passion if he didn't care for her.

He waited so long to answer she feared he was about to lie. "You already know what I feel."

She closed her eyes in gratitude. "I do know." Now that he'd admitted the truth, she felt confident enough to continue. "Once we're married—"

"Married?" He half rose from his seat, his voice harsh with shock.

His reaction jolted her. When two people loved each other, marriage seemed to be the next step. And really, given she was already over thirty, there was no reason to wait. Especially if they intended to start a family, which she sincerely hoped they would. The sooner the better.

"I assumed...I hoped," she faltered, then blushed when she realized he might not consider marriage necessary. "I'm afraid that if we don't legally marry, my brother will object. I...I would, however, defy him, if that were…necessary.'' But she prayed with all her heart it wouldn't be.

Laredo stood up and walked over to the railing, holding on to it, his back ramrod-straight with tension. ''I won't marry you, Savannah.''

Her heart sank as she absorbed the firm conviction in his statement. ''I see,'' she said, struggling to hide her disappointment. ''As I said earlier, while marriage would offer certain advantages, I'm willing to forgo the… legalities.''

He whirled around. ''Savannah, dear God in heaven, don't you understand what I'm saying?'' He knelt in front of her, his eyes wide with pain. ''It isn't that I *won't* marry you. I can't.''

''Can't?'' The awful possibility dawned. ''Are you…do you already have a wife?''

''No.''

She brought both hands to her heart in a gesture of relief.

''Look at me!'' he demanded. ''I don't have a pot to piss in. I don't have one damn thing to give you. Do you honestly think I'd take you away from your home, your family and friends, your roses and everything else to live in a *trailer?* Because that's all I've got—a lousy trailer.''

Feeling his pain, his inadequacy, she touched his cheek lovingly. ''Do you think it matters to me where we live? As for my garden, I can start another. You're all I need, all I'll ever need.''

He closed his eyes. ''Savannah, I can't. I'm sorry, but I can't.'' His hands squeezed hers with enough strength to make her fingers ache.

''I'm offering you my heart, my love, my life,'' she said, her voice barely audible.

He claimed both her hands with his own, then turned

them over and pressed his lips to her palms. When he raised his head, his eyes held hers. "You'd give all this up for me?"

"I wouldn't be giving up anything, Laredo. I'd be gaining so much more."

THAT NIGHT Laredo sat up in his bunk, his back against the wall, his mind whirling. Savannah had almost made him believe it was possible for the two of them. He was well aware that she'd be the one to make all the sacrifices; while that didn't seem right or fair, she'd assured him of her willingness to do it. To do whatever was necessary for them to be together.

Laredo rested his head between his hands and dreamed with his eyes open. A growing sense of excitement, of possibility, grew within him. *He loved her.*

Richard strolled into the bunkhouse and threw himself down on the cot where he'd slept that first time. Some nights he slept in the house; Laredo wished this was one of them. He supposed it depended on whether or not Grady was in the house and likely to notice. Despite her older brother's insistence, Laredo knew Savannah would never make Richard leave. She'd even let him stay in his boyhood room, perhaps allowing herself to believe that everything was all right again. Other nights, Richard slept in the bunkhouse. Grady must be around this evening.

"Hey, what're ya doing?" Richard asked.

"Thinking," Laredo answered shortly, hoping Weston would take the hint.

"So you're trying to steal Savannah away from us."

How did Richard know? "Do you have a problem with that?" Laredo demanded, suspicious of the other man's intentions.

"None whatsoever." Richard's hands flew up and he

grinned broadly. "As long as you love her," he added in melodramatic tones.

"I do." Not until the words escaped his lips did Laredo realize he had no problem telling Richard how he felt, although he'd never once told Savannah he loved her, not in so many words, at least.

"Ain't love grand," Richard said with an exaggerated sigh. He flopped back on the cot and gazed up at the ceiling. "At least in the beginning."

Laredo let the comment slide, although it hit its mark. Bull's-eye. What started out beautiful could often end up a disaster.

"Savannah's a real sweetheart," Richard continued. "Did you notice how hard she worked cooking for the party? Actually, if I know my sister, she was grateful to stay in the kitchen. It's always been difficult for her to deal with crowds, even people she's familiar with and known most of her life. I don't know why she's so damn shy. Take her out of her element and she wilts like a flower without water."

Laredo frowned, wondering if Richard was actually delivering a subtle message, one he would deny if asked, but would gleefully recount as an I-told-you-so if it came to pass.

"If you have something to say, then just say it," Laredo muttered.

"Me?" Richard's voice echoed his surprise. "I'm not saying anything other than how pleased I am for the two of you."

"Nothing's been decided." Laredo wanted to correct that impression right off.

Richard rolled his head to one side to get a better look at Laredo. "Really?"

"Really."

"Well, if everything goes as planned, it'll be wonderful. I know she'll make you happy, and once the kids start coming…"

"Kids?" The word exploded from Laredo's lips before he thought to censor it. They wouldn't be able to afford kids for years, although he knew Savannah was eager for a family. He was, too, but it just wasn't going to be possible, not until he'd established himself, had some income he could count on.

"I wouldn't advise you to wait too long," Richard was saying. "Savannah's already over thirty. Apparently the older the woman the more likely the chance of complications." He shook his head wisely and sounded as if he knew what he was talking about.

"I hope you've got good health insurance," he added. "From what I've heard, having a baby costs thousands of bucks these days."

Health insurance? Laredo could barely afford to put food on the table, let alone worry about extras. He knew Savannah, too. If there were problems, she wouldn't let him know because she wouldn't want him to worry.

"What about her rose garden?" Richard asked next. "We both know how important that is to her."

"She's talked about moving part of it," Laredo responded, but his mind was still stuck on the possibility of something happening to Savannah, miles from town, with few friends or neighbors. The reality of what he was asking hit him hard. It sounded romantic and exciting—the two of them building a home together, breeding quarter horses—until he thought about the risks.

"Moving part of the garden," Richard repeated. "Great idea." He sat up, tapping one foot on the floor. "You be real good to my big sister now, you hear?" Clapping his hands together, Richard laughed. "Hey! I'll bet you want me to keep my mouth shut about this in front of Grady. Right?''

Laredo didn't answer. The next time he looked up Richard was gone, which was just as well. Savannah's brother had opened his eyes to a few home truths. While it was fine to dream about making Savannah his bride, a dream was all it would ever be. He couldn't take her away from everything she knew and loved, couldn't put her health and happiness at risk. One of them had to keep a level head, and it looked like the responsibility had fallen to him.

He loved her, but he couldn't marry her. *Wouldn't* marry her. As soon as it could be arranged, he'd get out of her life. For her own good, as well as his own.

A WEEK LATER, as Grady sat on Starlight and watched over the grazing herd, his thoughts grew dark and oppressive. Sometimes he could cast off these moods when they threatened. More often, like now, he couldn't. He worried more and more about Savannah; he wasn't sure what had happened to his sister, but she hadn't been herself. Not for days. Outwardly nothing seemed wrong; she was as pleasant and cordial as always. Still, the difference was there. It seemed as if the light had gone out of her eyes somehow. The joy he'd seen in her of late had vanished.

He was no expert when it came to romance, but the answer was obvious. Something had happened between her and Laredo, who seemed equally miserable. Clearly they'd suffered some sort of falling-out. It was bound to happen, Grady realized.

He hated to see his sister hurt, and it made him feel helpless. He had no idea what to do, what to say. He'd even considered talking to Caroline, this being a woman thing and all. Savannah's best friend might be able to see her through this disappointment.

If only he could talk to someone about Richard. He supposed Cal Patterson, as his closest friend, would be that person. And yet he felt embarrassed. Ashamed. He hardly knew how it had happened, but Richard had managed to sweet-talk his way back into the family. It hadn't taken long for Savannah to pick up where their parents had left off, Grady thought with some bitterness. She spoiled him, indulged his every whim, pandered to his wishes as if he deserved a hero's welcome.

Grady still wanted Richard off the ranch, but every time he got to the point of ordering him to leave, he found he couldn't. Either because of Savannah's pleading or his own sense of…what? Obligation? Family loyalty? Pity? The one thing Grady had insisted on was that Richard sleep in the bunkhouse, but his worthless brother had found a way to thwart even that.

It had started innocently enough, with Richard cleaning out his old bedroom, sorting through his things. Before long he'd started sleeping up there. Some nights, anyway; Grady never knew for sure. It was another way Richard kept him off balance.

Grady shifted his weight in the saddle, tired after a long day. Just when he was about to head back to the ranch, he noticed another rider approaching at a gallop.

Laredo Smith. He waited for the man to join him.

"Problems?" Grady inquired.

"Not really."

From the way he'd ridden out here Grady wondered if the house was on fire. "There's a reason you came to see me, isn't there?"

"There is."

Apparently Smith was having a difficult time spitting

out the words. He looked even worse than Savannah, pale and lifeless.

"You were right, Grady," he said without emotion. "Have been from the first."

Grady liked the way this conversation had started. With Richard pulling the wool over everyone's eyes, it felt good to be told he was right about something. "How do you mean?"

"About me."

Grady's smile faded. This wasn't what he wanted to hear, wasn't what he'd expected, either. "In other words, you're the thief Earl Chesterton suspected?"

"No." His denial was quick. "Not that."

Grady would have been disappointed had it been the truth. Smith had proved himself a hardworking and talented horseman, probably the best he'd ever hired. He still didn't trust him, though, especially where his sister was concerned, and because of that, Grady had made a point of being difficult, demanding, even unreasonable. Laredo hadn't responded in kind, not once, and in the process had earned Grady's respect.

"You claimed I wasn't good enough for Savannah," Laredo said bluntly.

Grady frowned. He really didn't like the turn this conversation had taken. "What's going on between you two?" he asked, eyes narrowed.

Laredo ignored the question. "I need a favor."

"You got it."

His immediate response appeared to surprise Smith. "You might not be so fast to agree once you hear it involves money."

Grady sobered; the wrangler was right. "How much?"

"I need a loan. Enough to pay for the repairs on my truck and get me to Oklahoma."

"Any particular reason you're anxious to be on your way now?"

Smith rested his hands on the saddle horn and averted his face. "I've got my reasons."

"I don't suppose those reasons have anything to do with my sister?"

"They might."

"You hurt her, Smith, and you'll regret it." Grady was torn. On the one hand, Savannah's happiness seemed to depend on this man; on the other, he'd prefer to see Smith leave, get clear away from her. Grady suspected Smith's departure would come too late, that Savannah was already in too deep, emotionally committed to a drifter.

"Why the hell do you think I need that money so damned bad?" Laredo asked savagely. "The sooner I'm out of her life the better. Listen, I don't expect you to give me that loan without collateral. I'll leave the title to my truck with you until I can pay you back. Agreed?"

Grady mulled it over, not the decision to lend Laredo money—he had no problem with that—but why, exactly, Laredo seemed so anxious to leave. He sighed. He wasn't sure if he should interfere in the man's private affairs; he certainly wouldn't have appreciated anyone meddling in his.

"Agreed?" Laredo said again.

"There's another way," Grady said thoughtfully. Laredo stared at him long and hard before Grady continued. "You could stay here. I'll make you an offer that'll make it worth your while. A partnership—you and me and Savannah. I understand you're interested in breeding quarter horses. You could do that here on the Yellow Rose just as well as in Oklahoma."

Either Laredo was speechless at the offer or he was shocked that Grady knew this much about him and his plans. Grady credited Wiley for the information. His foreman had a loose tongue.

"If you're trying to bribe me into staying, all I can say is you've insulted the finest woman I know."

"It isn't a bribe," Grady insisted, damning himself for his inability to say things the way he wanted. "All I'm trying to do is give you another option." He stopped and boldly met the other man's eyes. "You love my sister, don't you?"

"Loving Savannah doesn't have anything to do with the loan," Laredo said stiffly. "Look, I have almost nothing to bring to a marriage. Nothing that's *mine*, that I worked for. I can't give her the things she's used to and deserves to have. I won't ask her to give up what she's got here. And a partnership...well, there's no way I could buy into the Yellow Rose, so a partnership is charity, pure and simple. I work for what I get—I don't accept charity."

Laredo's anger seemed to burn itself out and he said, "That loan. Are you willing to give it to me or not?"

"It's yours if you want it, but—"

"I want it."

"All right," Grady said, and thrust out his hand. For the very first time he believed in Laredo's sincerity. For the first time he fully accepted that his sister had chosen a man who deserved her love. A man he respected. A man he'd misjudged.

Laredo gripped his hand, and not for the first time Grady noted the intense sadness in his eyes. Grady refused to let go, demanding Laredo's full attention. "Are you sure this is what you want?"

Laredo nodded. "I'm sure."

He rode off with the same urgency with which he'd approached.

Grady frowned, wishing there was something he could do. But he knew that neither Savannah nor Laredo would appreciate his intrusion in their lives. This was between them; they had to work it out themselves—or not.

Bad as he felt for both of them, he could do nothing.

LAREDO NOTED the number on the small single-story dwelling in a quiet neighborhood and glanced down at the address on the slip of paper. He was about to commit perhaps the most cowardly act of his life. But what else could he do?

He stepped out of the truck and walked down the narrow path to the front door, a long narrow box tucked under his arm. He hesitated briefly, then rang the doorbell. It didn't take long for someone to answer. Maggie Daniels's eyes lit up in delight when she saw who it was.

"Hi, Laredo!"

Caroline revealed no such pleasure. "What are you doing here?"

He removed his hat. "I need you to do something for me if you would."

Savannah's friend didn't invite him inside, and it was just as well. He wanted to leave now, immediately. As he'd told Grady, the sooner he was able to put some distance between Savannah and him, the better.

"Come in," Caroline finally said, unlocking the screen door.

Laredo declined. "Thanks, but this should only take a moment." He handed her the box. "Would you mind giving this to Savannah for me?"

"You can't do it yourself?"

"No, ma'am."

She didn't accept the box. "Why not?"

"I don't plan on seeing her again." Saying the words

created a terrible sense of loss. He might be convinced that leaving was for the best, but that didn't make it any easier. He'd gotten the loan from Grady, and after supper Wiley had driven him into town to pick up his truck. He'd said his goodbyes to everyone.

Everyone except Savannah.

Although he called himself every name in the book, he couldn't make himself do it. He couldn't look her in the eye and pretend he didn't love her, and that was the price she'd demand before he left. She'd insist he say it to her face and he wouldn't be able to.

It occurred to him as he drove away from Powell's Garage that this feeling of grief and fear and loss must be similar to what his father had experienced when he left for Vietnam all those years ago.

"Well, if you won't come in, I'll join you on the porch." Caroline opened the screen door and stepped outside. Maggie, dressed in purple pajamas, followed her mother.

"I'd be much obliged if you'd give this to Savannah for me." He repeated his request.

Caroline's smile was knowing. "You love her, don't you?"

Laredo couldn't have denied it if he'd tried. "Sometimes love isn't enough."

"Really." She crossed her arms and walked to the porch railing and stared into the night sky. "Don't you think Savannah deserves to have you give her that gift yourself?"

"She deserves a great deal more than I can ever give her."

Caroline turned and faced him, leaning against the railing.

"What's in the package, Mommy?" Maggie asked.

"A gift for Savannah," her mother answered.

"Can I see?"

Laredo opened the box. As a parting gift and a token of love, it wasn't much, but it was all he could afford. "It's a shawl." He brought it out to show the little girl.

When Caroline saw the antique white silk threaded with gold strands, she sighed in appreciation. "It's perfect for her."

He was tempted to smile. He'd realized the same thing when he noticed it in the window of Dovie's shop. Instantly, he'd pictured Savannah sitting on the porch, the shawl wrapped around her shoulders. He'd never thought of himself as romantic, but in some small way he hoped that when she wore it, she'd feel his love. He hoped she'd understand that even though he'd left her, he would always love her.

"I know I'm asking a lot of you," Laredo said to Caroline.

"No," she replied. "The one you're asking a lot of is Savannah."

He recognized the truth of that immediately.

"Like I said," Caroline went on, "she deserves to have you give her this gift."

He shook his head. "I can't. Either you do it or I'll mail it."

Caroline hesitated. "Is there any message to go with it?"

He shook his head. He'd already said more than he'd intended.

"Nothing, Laredo?" Her eyes begged him not to be so cruel.

"Tell her..." His throat felt thick.

"Yes?"

"Tell her thank-you." He set his hat back on his head and hurried down the walkway.

Maggie tugged at her mother's sleeve. "Where's Laredo going?"

"I don't know, sweetheart. Laredo!" Caroline called to him.

He looked back.

"How'd you manage to pay for the repairs to your truck?"

He stood silent, refusing to answer her.

It didn't take Caroline long to figure it out. "Grady. He lent you the money, didn't he?" She leaped down the porch steps and planted her hands on her hips. "That son of a—" She bit off the last word.

Laredo climbed into his truck and started the engine, desperate to leave before he found an excuse to stay.

Chapter Ten

"What do you mean Laredo's gone?" Savannah didn't understand what Caroline was telling her. He'd been on the ranch earlier that day; she'd seen him herself. They'd both made an effort in the past week to pretend their discussion had never taken place. But it had, and her declaration of love stood between them. It was something they could neither forget nor ignore.

Every time Savannah thought about the foolish way she'd exposed her heart, she grew weary with self-recriminations and regret. Her rash behavior had embarrassed them both, yet she realized she probably couldn't have kept silent any longer. She loved Laredo, and hiding her feelings had become increasingly more difficult.

"He asked me to give you this," Caroline said with a regretful sigh, handing her a rectangular box.

"It's really pretty!" Maggie added enthusiastically.

"You've talked to him?" Savannah said. The pain was immediate. Laredo had left, and instead of coming to her, he'd gone to Caroline. He'd talked to Caroline, but not to her. He'd left without even a goodbye.

"He was on his way out of town when he stopped by and asked if I'd give you this."

Savannah felt an overwhelming need to sit down.

Slowly sinking onto a kitchen chair, she brought her fingers to her mouth to suppress a cry. *Laredo isn't coming back.*

"Do you want me to open the box for you, Savannah?" Maggie volunteered, eagerly lifting a corner of the box as she spoke. "It's so pretty and you're going to like it. Mommy did and so did I."

Caroline restrained her daughter by placing her hand on Maggie's shoulder. "Let Savannah open it when she's ready, okay, sweetheart?"

The child looked disappointed, but she nodded.

Savannah slid her fingers over the top of the box, but lacked the courage to look inside. All her strength went into holding back the tears that burned her eyes.

Laredo was gone. Without a word of farewell, without a note. Nothing. The pain of his leaving had devastated her. But in some odd inexplicable way she understood why he'd left so abruptly.

Laredo Smith *couldn't* say goodbye. He loved her too much to hurt her more. Loved her too much to refuse if she'd asked him to stay. And so he'd done the only thing he could. He'd slipped away like a thief in the night; he'd stolen her heart and taken it with him.

"Savannah, are you all right?"

She nodded even as she felt swallowed up in the emptiness.

Caroline's fingers gripped hers tightly. "I'm so sorry," she whispered.

Somehow Savannah managed to look at her friend. She could lie and offer reassurances, but she hadn't the strength to maintain a facade. It would be easy enough to fool Grady and Richard, but not Caroline.

"It's a shawl," Maggie blurted, unable to hold back any longer. "A pretty white one with gold—"

"Maggie," Caroline snapped.

The little girl lowered her head and bit her lip.

"A shawl... How nice," Savannah said, struggling. Knowing Maggie was impatient for her to open the gift, she pulled off the lid. The child was right; the shawl was quite possibly the loveliest one she'd ever seen. Lifting it from the tissue paper, she let the delicate fabric slide across her fingers. "Was there...did he give you any message for me?"

Caroline hesitated, then said gently, "He wanted me to thank you."

Her heart was breaking, the pain raw and real, and yet—despite the emotional intensity of the moment—Savannah smiled.

"Thank you." She repeated his message. This, too, she understood. The simple words held a wealth of meaning and in some ways were more valuable to her than the gift he'd asked Caroline to deliver.

Despite his desertion, Laredo had thanked her for loving him. Even though he'd walked out of her life with the same suddenness with which he'd entered it, he'd wanted Savannah to know her love had touched him. He couldn't say it himself, so he let someone else say it for him.

Caroline's eyes flashed with anger. "I don't understand why he'd do such a thing! He admitted he loved you—he said as much."

"I know."

"But when I asked why he was leaving, all he'd say was that sometimes love wasn't enough—whatever the hell that means." Caroline sat down, then got to her feet again and started pacing.

Savannah didn't try to explain. What Laredo apparently didn't grasp, and what she'd been unable to make him believe, was that his love was the one thing she'd ever need.

He seemed to think a prosperous ranch would make her happy, or a million head of cattle. A luxurious ranch house. A rose garden. Those things gave her security and contentment, true. But Laredo's love gave her happiness, and it gave meaning to everything else in her life. She'd tried to convince him that she'd happily work at his side, that their love would allow them to create a new security and contentment of their own. Why couldn't he believe her?

"Can I go sit on the swing outside?" Maggie asked.

Caroline nodded. "Stay on the porch."

Maggie assured Caroline she would, and the screen door slammed behind her. Caroline brewed Savannah a cup of strong coffee, then brought it over to the table. "Drink this," she ordered. "You look pale as a sheet."

Savannah raised the cup to her lips. Surprisingly the coffee revived her.

Caroline poured herself a cup and sat down next to Savannah. "I know you probably don't want to hear this at the moment, but I'm going to say it, anyway." She paused long enough to inhale deeply. "Right now, you're hurting too much to believe that everything happens for a reason. I don't know why, but that's the way it seems to work.

"When I discovered I was pregnant with Maggie, I felt as if the world had caved in on me. I was young and stupid and determined not to let a mistake ruin my life. First I thought the father would marry me, but...well, that was impossible. I'd already decided I wanted to have this baby, so I was left to deal with the pregnancy alone."

In all the years they'd been friends, this was the first

time Caroline had discussed anything to do with Maggie's birth. Or Maggie's father.

"When I couldn't hide that I was pregnant any longer, I had to tell my mother. I expected her to be furious, to call me all the names I'd called myself. Instead, Mom asked me a few questions and then held me. We both cried.

"It was what I'd needed most—her love. She talked about how difficult it must have been for me to keep this pain bottled up inside me all those weeks. I didn't want to tell her about Maggie's father, but I did, and how stupid I'd been to think he actually loved me..." Her voice wavered and it was a moment before she could continue. "You see, Savannah," she whispered with emotion shining in her eyes, "this mistake was really a gift. I made a mistake, but *Maggie's* not a mistake. She's my heart and my joy. I can't imagine life without her."

The screen door opened just then, and Maggie flew into the room and raced across the kitchen. Breathless, she wrapped her arms around Caroline's leg, hiding her face against her mother's jeans.

Grady followed her inside, looking frustrated and confused.

"What'd you do this time?" Caroline demanded.

"Not a damn thing," Grady said. "I saw Maggie outside and thought it was time the two of us talked, but it seems she's not ready."

Maggie clung to her mother's leg all the harder.

"It'd help if you hadn't yelled at her on the phone," Caroline suggested calmly.

"How was I supposed to know it was Maggie?" he shouted in return.

"He's yelling again," Maggie surfaced long enough to announce.

"Explain to her that it was all a mistake, would you?" Grady said in a strained voice, gesturing at Maggie. "She's right, I was a beast. But I'm willing to be a prince, too, if she'll give me the chance."

"You're too mean to be a prince," Maggie said next. Breaking away from her mother, she climbed into Savannah's lap and locked both arms around her neck. "I don't like Grady 'cause he yells."

"He's not one of my favorite people, either," Caroline said, glaring at Savannah's brother.

"What'd I do *now?*" he groaned. "Damn, but it's hard to understand women. I haven't talked to you in days— what could I possibly have done to offend you?"

"You know very well what you've done."

Clearly perplexed, he shrugged. "I'm afraid you're going to have to tell me, because I haven't got a clue."

"You're lower than a…a worm," Caroline said.

"So what else is new?" Grady sounded bored.

"Caroline?" Savannah said her friend's name softly, confused by the display of anger. "What did Grady do?"

Still glaring at him, Caroline crossed her long legs. Her foot swung with a furious rhythm. "I wasn't going to tell you," Caroline said, speaking to Savannah, "but you'll figure it out soon enough. Grady gave Laredo the money so he could pay off the repairs on his truck."

Savannah felt as if she'd been punched, as if the air had been forced from her lungs. She looked at her brother in shock and pain and disbelief. The abruptness of Laredo's leaving was almost more than she could bear, but knowing that her own *brother,* her own flesh and blood, had made it possible—had no doubt *encouraged* it—was like a knife in the back. She gasped. "Grady?"

"I didn't *give* him the money," Grady said, and his gaze darted between her and Caroline as if he didn't understand what he'd done that was so wrong. "I *lent* him the money."

He'd betrayed her.

There was nothing more to say.

Barely aware of what she was doing, Savannah stood and slowly placed one foot in front of the other. Hardly knowing how she'd managed it, she climbed the stairs to her room, dragging herself one step at a time.

"What'd I do that was so terrible?" her brother shouted after her. "Tell me, Savannah! I want to know!"

"Leave her alone," Caroline said angrily, her voice drifting toward Savannah as she climbed the stairs. "If you can't figure it out, trust me, I'll be happy to fill in the blanks. And you know what? I'll use small words so you'll be sure to understand."

GRADY DELAYED speaking to Caroline about Laredo for ten days. He knew he needed to say something—to explain, to talk about Savannah, to ask her advice. He saw her enter the Winn-Dixie one evening and followed her inside. He didn't want Caroline to assume he'd sought her out; he intended her to believe their meeting was accidental.

Taking a cart and maintaining a safe distance behind her, he trailed her into the produce section. Savannah was the one who did all the grocery shopping, and other than picking up a necessary item now and again, he was rarely in the supermarket.

He paused in front of a pyramid display of bright juicy-looking oranges, and with one eye on Caroline and the other on the task at hand, he reached for an orange. To his horror, the entire display collapsed.

Grady saw it happen as if in slow motion. He attempted to catch as many as possible before they tumbled to the floor, his arms moving frantically in every which direction. In the end he abandoned the effort, kneeling on the linoleum floor surrounded by fruit.

Everyone in the produce department stopped and stared at him. Even small children pointed and snickered. Grady smiled weakly and searched for a witty remark, but like everything else these past few weeks, his wit failed him.

He was about to turn tail and run when Caroline squatted down beside him. "This is another fine mess you've created, Grady Weston."

He didn't need Caroline to tell him that. If he wanted to make a fool of himself, he wouldn't choose to do it in front of half the store. Nope, he preferred to manage that with just one or two onlookers. Like Caroline. And his sister.

Together they gathered the spilled oranges and set them back on the display case. "Is there a reason you followed me in here?" she asked bluntly.

"Was I that obvious?"

"Don't apply to the Secret Service, all right?"

Since it was entirely obvious that running into her hadn't been an accident, he got straight to the point.

"Do you have time for coffee?" he asked, and then because he was afraid she might think he was asking her out, he added, "I'm worried about Savannah. I'd feel better if I talked about this with someone."

She checked her watch, and Grady had the feeling time wasn't her major concern. "Talked about this with just anyone?" she asked.

"With you," he amended, burying his pride. He owed Caroline this much.

"Let me phone the day care," she said, "and then I'll meet you at the bowling alley."

"Okay. See you there in a few minutes." He was eager to make his escape before he toppled a display of something *really* embarrassing—like feminine hygiene products.

The café in the bowling alley served some of the best food in town. It was certainly the most reasonably priced, with coffee only a quarter a cup. They served decent coffee, too. There was always a special; according to the reader board outside, today's was T-bone steak and a baked potato. And the place stayed open all night on weekends. In Grady's opinion, it was a damn good deal. Although he wasn't interested in a steak at the moment.... Even if he'd been hungry, he couldn't have choked it down.

Arriving first, he found an empty booth and turned over two mugs. The waitress brought him a couple of menus and smiled. "Haven't seen you in a while, Grady."

"Hello, Denise. How're Art and the kids?" Grady had attended high school with Denise a hundred years ago. While he was out chasing cattle, his classmate had married, had three kids and started working here part-time.

"I can't complain. Billy's in junior high this year."

Hard to believe, Grady thought. Art and Denise's oldest boy was reaching his teens and *he* wasn't even married yet.

Denise filled his mug with coffee. "Are you going to order something to eat?"

"Not me, but Caroline might."

"Caroline Daniels?" Denise filled the second mug.

He nodded, disliking the flicker of interest in her eyes.

"Are you two seeing each other now?" she asked, her interest far too avid.

Grady opened his mouth to deny everything. He didn't have to.

"No way," Caroline answered for him as she slipped into the booth. She handed Denise the menu, effectively dismissing her, and reached for the sugar dispenser. "You had something you wanted to say about Savannah."

"Yeah." This was more difficult than he'd imagined.

"Is she all right?" Caroline leaned back against the patched red vinyl upholstery, and he noted for the first time how pale she was. He didn't comment because sure as hell she'd make something of it—something he'd never intended. His only chance to have a peaceful conversation was to stick to the matter at hand and ignore everything else. Still, he wondered.

"How come you haven't been out to the ranch?" he blurted. His sister needed a friend, and he'd expected Caroline to be there for her, especially now.

"I stopped by a couple of times when you weren't around."

"On purpose?" he asked, thinking she'd taken to avoiding him because of Maggie.

"No, it just happened to work out that way. I haven't gone anywhere in a couple of days. I've been dealing with postal inspectors all week. I had my own crisis to handle, but fortunately that's behind me now." She cradled the mug between her hands. "I've phoned Savannah every day." Her eyes held his. "Is something going on with her that I don't know about?"

"Not with Savannah, exactly," he said, then looked away, finding her scrutiny uncomfortable. "First off, I was wrong about Laredo Smith."

That captured her attention, he could tell. She raised

her eyebrows but said nothing. Not yet, anyway. Naturally she'd delight in hearing how wrong he'd been.

"I should have accepted Savannah's assessment of his character," Grady said, embarrassed that he'd allowed his fears to get in the way. Admitting he'd made a mistake had never come easy. "I...came to some, well, erroneous conclusions about Smith. The result was that he and I got started on the wrong foot."

"You should tell Savannah this, not me."

"I have!" he snapped, then took a deep breath in an effort to control his impatience. When he spoke again, he lowered his voice. "I did tell her, but I wanted you to know, as well."

"Should I be grateful?"

Grady decided to ignore the sarcasm. "Laredo came to me and asked for a loan. Despite what you think, I'm not blind. I knew something wasn't right. I didn't want him to leave and I told him so."

This appeared to surprise Caroline. Her eyebrows rose again. "You did?"

"Yes—not that it did any good. In the end I agreed to lend him the money and he insisted on giving me the title to his truck. The day he left I apologized for the scene at Richard's party and we shook hands." He stared into the steaming mug. "I took my aggravation with Richard out on Laredo and made a complete ass of myself."

Caroline didn't disagree with him. Not that he expected she would.

"Although it's none of my business," he said, "Laredo as much as admitted he loved Savannah."

"He told me that, too." Caroline shook her head in dismay. "What I can't fathom is why he felt he had to leave. What is it about men? I don't understand it. Laredo Smith is loved by the sweetest, kindest, most wonderful woman he's likely to meet in ten lifetimes and what does he do? He walks out on her without a word. It doesn't make sense." She tossed her hands in the air as if to say she'd never understand the male of the species.

"A man has his pride, especially a man like Smith, but my guess is Richard had something to do with it." It was the first time he'd suggested this to anyone, and he was curious to see how Caroline would react. He half expected her to jump all over him and insist he quit trying to blame Richard for everything, including the national debt. She said nothing for several moments.

"I wouldn't put it past him," she murmured at last.

Grady was so damn grateful that she agreed with him it was all he could do not to hug her right then and there. If Denise was going to spread rumors about him and Caroline, *that* would give her something to talk about.

"Did you ask Laredo if Richard said anything to him?"

"No," he told her reluctantly.

"Why the hell not?"

"Well, because...I was trying to get him to stay." Grady didn't know what Caroline had thought he could do. It wasn't like he could hog-tie the wrangler until he agreed to marry his sister. Grady hadn't intended to tell Caroline this, but suddenly he wanted her to know. "I offered Laredo a partnership in the ranch. I realize now it must have come as quite a surprise to him. Hell, I surprised myself."

He'd already known Savannah was in love with Laredo; that day he'd learned about Smith's love for Savannah, too. This man was important to her happiness; if it was in Grady's power to make her happy, he was willing to do whatever it took.

He noticed how Caroline's face tightened as she considered this information. "What'd he say to that?"

Glancing away, Grady relived the terse conversation. "That he didn't accept charity and I'd insulted Savannah and him. Hell, everything I do these days is wrong. I was only trying to help." He reached for his coffee. "At first I thought Laredo didn't love Savannah, but now I think he loves her too much."

Caroline gave a hard shake of her head. "As far as I'm concerned, he'd better not show his face around here, because I swear I'll wring his neck if he does."

Grady was a little taken aback by the vehemence of her response.

"All this crap about pride and honor—it's asinine, that's what it is." Her lips thinned. "Never mind him. How's Savannah doing?"

"You said you haven't seen her in the past couple of days, didn't you?"

Caroline nodded. "Why? What's up?"

"Something's happened—she's changed."

"Of course she's changed! She's hurt and angry. And I can't blame her."

"It's more than that."

Caroline leaned closer. "What do you mean?"

"Like you said, she's hurt—but I can't imagine how that would lead to…this." He didn't know how to say it without sounding demented, so he just plunged in. "Hell, I don't know what's happened to her, but two days ago she cut her hair."

"Savannah?"

"It's been long for so many years I didn't recognize her. It's shoulder-length now and in a—" he made a circular motion with his finger "—pageboy, I think is what you call it. The ends tuck under sort of nice and neat.''

This left Caroline speechless.

"Then yesterday I found her in jeans."

"Savannah?"

"Yeah. I didn't know she even owned any."

"But why?" Caroline asked, clearly puzzled. "Why'd she do these things?"

"I have my suspicions and I'll tell you right now, it makes my blood run cold."

"Really," Caroline said thoughtfully, "when you think about it, what's so terrible about Savannah cutting her hair and updating her wardrobe?"

"I'm worried." Grady didn't mind admitting it, either. "This morning I saw her standing on the porch looking down the driveway as if she expected Laredo to come back. Personally I wish to hell he would, but I don't think it's going to happen."

"I hope you didn't tell her that!"

"Of course not!" What kind of idiot did Caroline think he was, anyway? "Then she told me Laredo Smith was a fool," he added.

"I couldn't agree with her more," Caroline muttered.

"You know what I think? I think Savannah's decided to look for a husband." He spoke quickly, finding the subject of marriage an uncomfortable one with Caroline.

Caroline gave an elaborate shrug. "There's nothing wrong with marriage, although neither of *us* seems interested in it."

"I agree—nothing wrong with it. But I'm afraid that in Savannah's current frame of mind any man will do."

"Did she have someone in mind?"

"Not that I'm aware of." But Grady knew his sister, and while he wasn't an expert, he recognized the look.

Savannah was on the prowl. And when a woman set her mind on marriage, he believed, there was damn little a man could do but run for shelter.

"You're sure about this?" Caroline frowned.

"Not a hundred percent, but it's fairly obvious."

Then to his consternation, Caroline burst out laughing.

Grady didn't take kindly to being the butt of a joke. "What's so damned funny?" he demanded.

"You! I don't think Savannah's on the prowl, as you put it, but if she does find a decent man to marry, more power to her. There's too much love in her heart to waste. If Laredo doesn't want to marry her, then so be it. Eventually she'll find a man who does."

"In some tavern?"

"Savannah's not into that scene."

"That's what I thought, but then Richard..." Grady hesitated, uncertain he should tell her this, but if Caroline could help...

"What about Richard?" she asked, her laughter draining away quickly.

It helped that his no-good brother hadn't fooled Caroline, that she recognized the kind of man he was. "Richard offered to take her barhopping and introduce her around."

"Terrific," Caroline said sarcastically. "All the best men hang around bars. Is she going to do it?"

"I don't know," Grady said. "I just don't know."

GLEN PATTERSON sat down in front of the television with a cold can of soda. He was supposed to meet Ellie for dinner, but she'd phoned and said she'd be hung up until after seven. This was a difficult time for his friend. Twice this week he'd made excuses to drive into town and check up on her. The last report he'd heard on her father wasn't good. The doctors seemed to think John Frasier wouldn't last more than another week or two.

"You're frowning," Cal said as he stepped into the living room. It wasn't as neat and orderly as when their mother had done the housekeeping, but it wasn't as bad as it might've been, either. The two brothers had hired a woman to come in once a week to clean ever since their parents had retired and moved into town to open a bed-and-breakfast.

"I was just thinking," Glen said.

"Worried about Ellie?"

"Not really." He downplayed his concern rather than admit it to his brother.

"Maybe you *should* be worried," Cal said as he claimed the recliner. He sat down and stretched out his long legs.

"Do you know something I don't?"

Cal didn't look at him when he spoke. "I hear Richard Weston's got his eye on her."

"Richard? He's harmless. Okay, so he likes to flirt, but Ellie knows that."

"You jealous?"

If anyone understood his relationship with Ellie, it should be his own brother. "Why would I be jealous? Ellie and I are friends. Nothing more. Nothing less."

Friends. It shouldn't be a difficult concept to understand. Cal and Grady Weston had been good friends for years. It just so happened that *his* best friend was a member of the opposite sex. People had been trying to make something of it for years.

Cal regarded him skeptically.

"What?" Glen asked in annoyance.

"Men and women can't be friends."

Glen had his older brother on that one. "Wrong. Ellie's like one of the guys. She always has been—you know that.''

Cal folded his hands over his trim stomach. ''In other words, it doesn't bother you she's been seeing Richard.''

''Not in the least.'' It did a little, but not enough to really concern him—and not for the reasons Cal might suggest. Glen was afraid that Ellie was especially vulnerable just then, and he didn't want Richard Weston to take advantage of her.

''You know how Grady feels about him,'' Cal said.

''Yeah, so what? Richard wasn't cut out to be a rancher—we both know that. He has a right to come home now and then, don't you think?''

Cal was silent for a moment. Then he said, ''If I were you, I'd keep my eye on Ellie.''

Glen found himself frowning again. Cal had a suspicious nature but he hadn't always been this cynical or distrusting. Glen traced it back to Jennifer Healy—Cal had been engaged to her a couple of years ago, and Jennifer had dumped him. Afterward Cal's disposition had soured, particularly toward women. It bothered Glen and he'd tried a number of times to steer his older brother into a new relationship, but Cal didn't seem interested.

''Well, I know for a fact that Richard can be a real bastard,'' Cal added. ''If you're Ellie's friend, like you say, you'd better warn her.''

''Warn?'' Obviously Cal hadn't been around her often enough. Ellie had a mind of her own and wouldn't take kindly to his interference.

Anyway, he just couldn't take Richard seriously as a threat. An annoyance, yes, but not a threat.

Chapter Eleven

As Savannah drove toward Bitter End, she considered the unmistakable fact that her family was worried about her. She'd shocked everyone by cutting her hair, no one more than herself. The decision had come on the spur of the moment, without warning or forethought.

She'd been washing her face as she did each morning and happened to catch her reflection in the bathroom mirror. For a long moment, she'd stood there staring.

How plain she looked. How ordinary. Carefully, critically, she examined her image and didn't like what she saw. That was when she decided something had to be done. Anything. Not until she reached for the brush did she consider cutting her waist-length blond hair. One minute she was staring in the mirror, the next she had a pair of scissors in her hands.

Savannah knew she'd shocked Grady and Wiley that first morning. They'd come into the kitchen for breakfast and stopped cold, unable to keep their mouths from sagging open. Her brother squinted and looked at her as if she were a stranger. Not that Savannah blamed him. She *felt* like a stranger.

Naturally Grady, being Grady, had simply ignored the change after that and didn't say a word. Frowning, he sat down at the table and dished up his breakfast as though there was nothing out of the ordinary. And Wiley, being Wiley, couldn't resist commenting. He approved of the change and said so, forcing Grady to agree with him.

Savannah began to like her new look. Everything that followed after she'd cut her hair was a natural progression of this first action. She'd worn the ankle-length dresses for comfort and out of habit. The jeans were leftovers from her high school days and, surprisingly, still fit.

Of the three men Richard had been the most complimentary about the new Savannah. Her younger brother had done his best to flatter and charm her. To his credit his efforts had made her laugh, something she hadn't done in quite a while. She worried about Richard and his finances, but again and again he assured her the check would be coming soon. The one who surprised her most was Grady. It was as if he'd forgotten about Richard, but her younger brother was smart enough to avoid him. He spent his evenings in town, and while Grady was out working, Richard practiced his guitar or serenaded her. The past few afternoons he'd joined her on the porch to keep her company. It helped distract her from thoughts of Laredo, and Savannah was grateful. A couple of times he'd attempted to talk her into going to town with him to, as he put it, live it up a little. He seemed to believe that all she needed was a new love interest. Another man, who'd take her mind off Laredo.

What Richard didn't understand was that she couldn't turn her feelings on and off at will. He prodded her, claiming it would lift her spirits to get out and circulate. While she appreciated his efforts, she wasn't ready. In truth she didn't know if she would ever be. Not that she intended to mourn the loss of her one and only love for the remainder of her days. She'd given herself time to accept that Laredo was out of her life; after that, she was determined to continue on as she had before.

Easier said than done.

Savannah's hands clenched the steering wheel as she came to a particularly bumpy stretch of road. Although she knew Grady highly disapproved of her going back to the ghost town, she'd decided to do it, anyway.

Not because of the roses, either, She'd already discovered, the day Laredo had come with her, that no other flowers were to be found there, old roses or otherwise. The land was completely barren. Nevertheless, she felt compelled to return for one last visit.

Her reason was nebulous, hard to analyze or explain. But Savannah didn't care. The why of it no longer concerned her. She felt drawn in some indefinable way to this lifeless empty town.

She was pitched and jolted around as she drove slowly toward Bitter End. Oddly, the truck seemed to remember each turn, and she followed without question, parking in the same spot and hiking the rest of the way.

As she neared the place, the memories of her last visit with Laredo immediately came to mind. For weeks now she'd managed to curtail her thoughts of him, telling herself it did no good to brood on might-have-beens; he was gone and nothing she said or did would bring him back. She had no choice but to accept his decision.

At least that was the sane and sensible approach. In reality it just hurt too damned much to linger over the memories.

Every time she stepped into her garden the first thing she saw were the trellises he'd built for her. The roses he'd fertilized and cared for had exploded with fresh blooms. She would cut and arrange them, knowing that his hands had touched these very stems.

It hadn't been easy. None of it.

Caroline worried about her, too, and phoned frequently to check on her. Rather than come right out and tell her she was concerned, her friend manufactured excuses for her calls. She still wasn't coming out to the ranch very often, but Savannah blamed Grady and his talent for frightening Maggie.

As she climbed onto the rocky ledge, Bitter End came into view. She stared at the church at the outskirts of town. The whole place looked peaceful and serene from here, and she wondered about the sadness and oppression she'd experienced on her last visit. Maybe it was her imagination, after all. Laredo's, too. He'd shared her uneasiness and hadn't been able to get her away fast enough.

But as she walked past the church and down the main street, the sensation returned. The feeling seemed to wrap itself around her, but Savannah refused to be intimidated. She wasn't going to run away.

Not this time.

She moved forward carefully and deliberately. The sidewalks had been built a good two to three feet off the ground and were lined with railings. A water trough, baked for a hundred years in the unyielding sun, sat by the hitching post. Savannah advanced toward it, thinking that, instead of walking down the center of the street as she had with Laredo, she'd take the sidewalk and explore a couple of buildings along the way.

Just then she heard a bird's mournful cry reverberating in the stillness. The wind whistled, a keening sound, as though someone was grieving some great loss. Sagebrush tumbled down the hard dirt street. She stopped, looking around, and realized there was something different.

"The rocking chair," she said aloud. She was certain no chair had been there before. But now one stood outside the mercantile store, creaking in the wind, and her heart lodged in her throat.

Determined not to give in to the fear that sent goose bumps skittering up her arms, she strolled fearlessly ahead. Her bravado didn't help. The feeling of dread persisted.

In that instant she understood. It was an emotional understanding and it told her why she'd come, what had driven her back to the ghost town. Standing in the middle of town, she looked up and down the barren street and saw nothing but tumbleweeds and dust.

The street was stark. Empty. Bare. Even the land refused to nurture growth.

This town, this lifeless unproductive street, was like her life. She lived holed up on the ranch with her unmarried brothers. Her entire life revolved around their needs, their wants, their demands.

Her roses and her mail-order business were tolerated, but no one had offered her one word of encouragement. Except Laredo. Grady cared about her; she didn't mean to belittle his concern. But he hadn't the time or energy to invest in understanding her or her needs. As for Richard, although she loved him, she knew he'd never been able to look past his own interests.

Until Laredo, her existence had been empty. Outwardly focused, with no regard for her own happiness, her own growth. *Before Laredo. After Laredo.* Savannah smiled to herself. It seemed her entire life would now be divided into two parts. Before he'd come and after he'd left.

How odd that she'd find herself smiling like that. Just when she'd recognized her life for what it was. Shallow. Without a center.

The restlessness she'd held at bay all this time felt as though it would crush her. Ignoring the unhappiness had done no good. Repressing it hadn't worked. For weeks she'd been fighting headaches and listlessness. For weeks her body had tried to tell her what standing alone in the ghost town had finally made her understand.

She saw a small corral across from the hotel, a large rock beside it. Savannah walked over and sat there, trying to assimilate what she'd learned about herself.

A memory came to her. One she'd long forgotten. She'd been barely ten when her father had been tossed from his horse. He'd badly broken his leg but had somehow managed to crawl to safety and avoid further injury.

Savannah remembered how her mother, frightened and ashen-faced, had run to his side and held his hand while she drove him to the clinic. Mel Weston had smiled and, between deep breaths, assured his wife that the pain told him he was still alive.

That was what this pain told Savannah. She was alive. She could still feel and love and be. Laredo had taught her that, and so much more. For the first time in her adult life, she recognized how much love her heart could hold.

No matter how much it hurt, she'd do it all again.

She bowed her head against the wind as it blew sagebrush about her feet. Tears filled her eyes, but they weren't the same tears that had burned her face in weeks past.

Savannah had made peace with herself.

GRADY NOTICED a difference in Savannah the minute she got out of the truck. Her face radiated a serenity, an acceptance, one that had clearly been hard-won.

His sister hadn't told him where she was going, but Grady could guess and he hadn't liked it. Not one damn bit. How she'd come away from Bitter End with any kind of tranquillity was beyond him. Half a dozen times he'd considered going after her and talked himself out of it, knowing Savannah wouldn't appreciate his interference.

She joined him in the kitchen and put on water for a pot of tea. "I'm going to be all right now," she told him.

Grady wasn't sure what to say. He'd wanted to talk to her about the last conversation he'd had with Laredo, wanted to comfort her, but he feared he'd do more harm than good.

"I won't be going back," she said next as she took the china teapot from the shelf above the stove. She didn't say where and he didn't ask.

"Good," was all Grady said, at a loss for words.

"Would you care for a cup of tea?" she asked, sounding almost like her old self.

Grady preferred dark strong coffee and Savannah knew it. The offer was more a gesture of reconciliation, an outstretched hand. "Tea sounds wonderful," he said.

Savannah smiled and brought down an extra cup and saucer.

In the days that followed, the transformation in his sister became more apparent. Color returned to her pale cheeks and a radiance to her face. She started to sing and hum once again and baked his favorite chocolate-chip cookies. Savannah was back, and yet it wasn't quite the same Savannah as before. These changes were very subtle.

His sister had always been a fearless advocate for people she believed in. Now she believed in herself, too. Her fledgling mail-order business took off like gangbusters once she finished her catalog. Orders poured in from across the country—surprising even Savannah, who'd barely got her catalog mailed out when the responses started to arrive, at a fast and furious pace. The fax machine was in constant use. She soon became known as an expert on old roses and two awards came in quick succession. First she was honored with the grand prize by the Texas Rose Society for one of her premiere roses, which she'd named Laredo's Legacy. The following day, she was asked to speak at next year's Rose Festival in Tyler, Texas, known as the rose capital of the world. Public speaking terrified Savannah, and Grady suspected she'd politely decline. To his amazement she accepted.

Grady wasn't the only one who noticed the changes in Savannah. Caroline did, too. Even Richard, self-centered as he was, commented on her new attitude. Grady was proud of her, exceptionally proud, and he wanted to let her know. He could think of only one way. He ordered her prize-winning rose, Laredo's Legacy, and together with Savannah, planted it at their parents' grave. Savannah had thanked him with tears shining in her eyes.

His sister, Grady realized, was quite possibly the most incredible woman he'd ever known. How odd that it had taken him so long to realize it.

Chapter Twelve

Humming softly to herself, Savannah checked the living room one last time to be sure everything was in place. Laredo had been gone more than six weeks now, and she'd stopped waiting for him, stopped dreaming he'd return. Her life had settled back into a comfortable groove, and the happiness she'd found with him would forever be part of her. That happiness, that sense of possibility, was what she chose to remember, rather than the emptiness she'd felt at his leaving.

It was Savannah's turn to host the women's group from church, and her nerves were fluttering. Within a couple of hours twenty women would crowd into the living room to plan a church dinner.

Earlier in the day she'd baked apple pies, and because Grady had been such a good sport about everything lately, she'd made a lemon meringue pie for him, too. The scent that lingered in the house was an enticing mixture of cinnamon, nutmeg and lemon.

"Is Caroline coming?" Grady asked, walking into the kitchen. Just as he was about to stick his finger into the lemon pie, she slapped his hand.

"You can have a piece later," she told him. "And, yes, Caroline's coming."

"What about Maggie?"

Savannah carried the pie to safety. "She'll be with Dovie Boyd."

"Dovie?" He sounded almost disappointed. "She's old enough to be Maggie's..."

"Grandmother," Savannah supplied. "Caroline's mother and Dovie were good friends, and Dovie likes to fill in as Grandma every now and again. Why are you so curious?"

He shrugged and strolled out of the kitchen. Savannah didn't have time to wonder about it. As soon as she finished the last of the dishes, she needed to shower and change clothes.

Two hours later the living room was filled with the chatter and laughter of women. Savannah handed out copies of her apple-pie recipe and refilled coffee cups from her mother's silver pot. She was joking with Millie Greenville from the flower shop when the room went strangely quiet. Everyone had turned to look behind Savannah. Certain Richard was up to one of his tricks, she turned around, too, ready to chastise him.

She froze.

Laredo stood in the doorway, his Stetson in his hand. He looked about as uncomfortable as a man could get—as though it was all he could do not to turn tail and run.

"Hello, Savannah," he said.

She couldn't have responded had her life depended on it. He looked travel-weary. His jacket was dusty and his face pale beneath his tan, but Savannah had never seen anyone more beautiful.

He seemed to be thinking the same thing about her because for that long, unbroken moment he didn't take his eyes off her.

"I can see I've come at a bad time," he said, glancing away from Savannah long enough to scan the room. All the women were openly curious about him; Savannah had never heard anything louder than this silence.

"You couldn't have come at a better time," Caroline insisted, leaping to her feet. "It looks to me like you'd appreciate a slice of Savannah's apple pie. Sit down and make yourself at home while I dish it up for you. Savannah'll see to your coffee."

A space magically appeared between two women sitting on the sofa. Savannah remained frozen, unable to breathe or think. This was unfair. Just when she'd forged a new path for herself, accepted his absence, he was back.

Unable to hide his discomfort, Laredo settled down between Nell Bishop and Ellie Frasier, looking as out of place as a junkyard dog sitting between toy poodles.

Caroline served him a huge slice of apple pie. "Perhaps you'd like to tell Savannah why you're here?" the postmistress asked pointedly.

The room fell silent again, awaiting Laredo's response. Every eye was on him. Including Savannah's. His gaze darted about the room, and he swallowed noticeably. "I've come to ask Savannah to be my wife."

The silver coffeepot in Savannah's hands suddenly weighed a hundred pounds, and she set it down on the silver platter with a clank. The buzz of voices surrounded her. Her heart raced and everything felt unreal.

At that precise moment Grady burst into the room. "Is that Laredo's truck parked in the yard with the horse trail—?" He came to an abrupt halt when he realized he'd walked into the middle of the church group.

"I believe it is," Caroline answered, gesturing toward Laredo.

The wrangler sprang to his feet, looking at Grady with unmistakable relief.

"What are you doing here?" Grady demanded.

Savannah wanted to stop him, to explain that Laredo had already been through one inquisition and that was enough, but she wasn't given the chance.

"I've come to ask your sister to marry me." Laredo answered as he had earlier, only this time there was a hint of challenge in his voice, as though he expected Grady to argue with him.

Again a murmur arose.

Edwina Moorhouse's old bones creaked as she stood and motioned at Laredo. "All right, young man, tell me what makes you think Savannah should marry you."

Color surged into Laredo's neck and crept upward. "I love her," he answered simply.

"So does everyone else in this room," Lily put in, following her sister's lead and standing up.

"And we're not about to let some stranger steal her away." This from Millie Greenville.

"That...that was one of the reasons I left," Laredo explained haltingly. "I didn't want to take Savannah from her home and family."

"How has that changed?"

Laredo motioned with his head toward Grady. "I decided to take her brother up on his offer."

"What offer?" Savannah asked, turning to regard her brother.

Grady had started to ease his way toward the kitchen. "Ah, perhaps we should talk about all this later. In private," he added pointedly.

"It's time for us to go," Caroline suggested. The ladies began to gather their purses, but Edwina called a stop to it.

"Now just a minute. I'm seventy-five and too old to go without my sleep. I can tell I'm not going to rest until I hear Savannah's answer. Do you love this man?" she asked, pointing at Laredo.

Savannah nodded.

"You're willing to marry him?"

Again she nodded, more forcefully this time.

"It's been a while since Wade performed a wedding ceremony," Nell Bishop piped up. Her mother-in-law agreed, trying to remember whose wedding that was.

"I always did love a summer wedding," Lily Moorhouse said, glancing from Laredo to Savannah.

"A wedding's just what this town needs," Louise Powell declared, as though that should be the last word on the subject.

But it wasn't. The group of delighted women became engaged in the conversation, exchanging ideas, offering suggestions. The level of noise and excitement rose perceptibly and wedding plans flew in all directions. Millie suggested white and pink roses for the bridal bouquet, but white calla lilies for the arrangement on the altar. Louise had strong opinions on the meal that should be served. Edwina recommended some musical selection.

Through all this Laredo's eyes remained locked with Savannah's, and it seemed to them that only the two of them were present. She felt his love; it warmed her, even from halfway across the room. His expression told her how miserable he'd been without her, how lonely. She knew that, like her, he'd struggled with the pain. He'd also struggled with pride. But in the end his love, *their* love, was stronger. Laredo Smith needed her as badly as she needed him.

"I do think we should leave now, don't you, ladies?" Caroline tried again, gathering up empty plates and cups.

A chorus of agreement followed this time, and everyone stood.

"Well, that's that," said Edwina. "Come on, Lily, if we hurry home we'll be in time for a game of cribbage before 'Jeopardy' comes on."

The room emptied more quickly than Savannah would have thought possible. She happily forgave Caroline for abandoning the stack of dishes. In less than a minute the crowd was out the door, and the sound of cars starting replaced the chatter of twenty women.

"You cut your hair," Laredo said now that they were alone. He stood half a room away from her, his hat in his hands.

Savannah raised her fingers to touch it.

"It looks wonderful." His voice dipped. "*You* look wonderful. You're more beautiful now than ever. I didn't think that was possible."

"You look wonderful, too." She smiled. "What happened?" she asked suddenly, the words rushing from her lips. "Why'd you go?"

"For all the wrong reasons. My pride, mainly, and my fear."

"Fear?"

"My mother told me I was a fool to have listened to...my doubts. I sold my land in Oklahoma," he said, "and brought Renegade with me. If you're agreeable, I'll accept Grady's offer to become a partner in the ranch. Renegade will be my stake, and in time the Yellow Rose will have the finest quarter horses in the country. I promise you that. I don't have a lot to offer you, not nearly as much as you deserve, but I love you, Savannah." He took a step closer. "I didn't realize how much until I reached Oklahoma. My land was there, my dream, and it meant nothing if you couldn't share it with me."

"I thought my life was over when you left," she whispered. "You didn't even say goodbye."

"I couldn't—but I swear I won't leave you again. Mom's right—I'm too much like her. I'll only love once in my life, and if I let you go, there won't be a second chance. I couldn't ask you to wait, but I realize now that I couldn't wait, either. I love you too much."

"I love you, too, so much... Why are you standing way over there when I'm right here?"

Laredo covered the space between them in three strides. None too soon she was in his arms. It was heaven to feel his lips on hers, warm, moist, hungry. His kiss told her everything. How much he wanted her, needed her. How much he loved her.

Savannah felt the steady beat of his heart beneath her palm and returned his kiss in full measure, clinging to him. Her heart was full enough to burst.

"Children?" she managed the question between kisses.

"As many as you want. Oh, Savannah, I can't wait for you to meet my mother. She loves you already." His arms tightened about her.

From behind them Grady cleared his throat loudly. "I take it everything's been decided?"

Laredo tucked his arm around Savannah's waist and held her close. "We're getting married as soon as it can be arranged."

"Good. I assume that's Renegade in the trailer?"

Laredo nodded. "I'm taking you up on your offer, Grady, but I want it understood right now that I'll pay my own way. I'm here because of Savannah, not because of anything you offered. Understand?"

Grady held up both his hands and grinned widely. "Understood."

"HOT DAMN," Richard said as he sauntered into the room, guitar slung over his shoulder. "You mean there's going to be a wedding in the family? Well, all I can say is better late than never!"

* * * * *

In March, join the people of Promise again and follow all their doings! In Texas Two-Step, Ellie Frasier falls in love—and two men seem to be in love with her. What about Grady and Caroline? Are they ever going to get along? And Richard—what's he up to? Come and visit Promise…and maybe even Bitter End, the mysterious ghost town. See you there next month!

HARLEQUIN PRESENTS

HARLEQUIN PRESENTS
men you won't be able to resist
falling in love with...

HARLEQUIN PRESENTS
women who have feelings
just like your own...

HARLEQUIN PRESENTS
powerful passion in
exotic international settings...

HARLEQUIN PRESENTS
intense, dramatic stories that will keep you
turning to the very last page...

HARLEQUIN PRESENTS
The world's bestselling romance series!

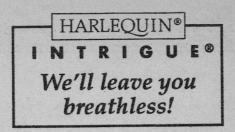

HARLEQUIN SUPERROMANCE®

...there's more to the story!

Superromance. A *big* satisfying read about unforgettable characters. Each month we offer *four* very different stories that range from family drama to adventure and mystery, from highly emotional stories to romantic comedies—and much more! Stories about people you'll believe in and care about. Stories too compelling to put down....

Our authors are among today's *best* romance writers. You'll find familiar names and talented newcomers. Many of them are award winners—and you'll see why!

If you want the biggest and best in romance fiction, you'll get it from Superromance!

Available wherever Harlequin books are sold.

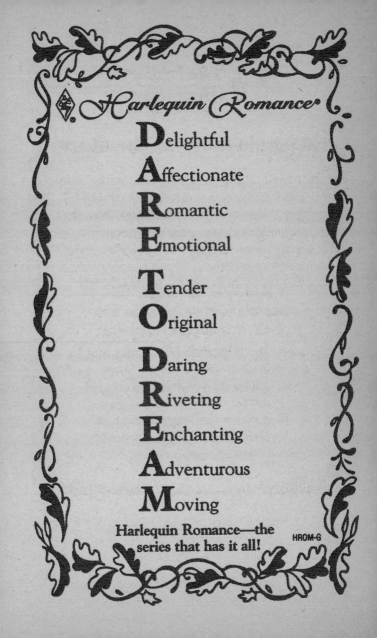

Harlequin Romance®

Delightful

Affectionate

Romantic

Emotional

Tender

Original

Daring

Riveting

Enchanting

Adventurous

Moving

Harlequin Romance—the
series that has it all!

HROM-G

Harlequin® Historical

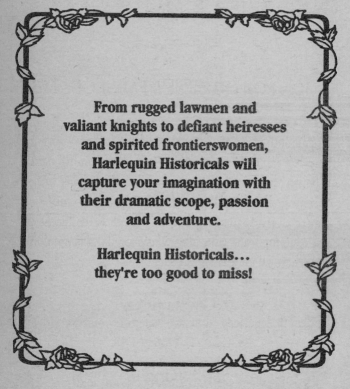

From rugged lawmen and
valiant knights to defiant heiresses
and spirited frontierswomen,
Harlequin Historicals will
capture your imagination with
their dramatic scope, passion
and adventure.

Harlequin Historicals...
they're too good to miss!

HHGENR

LOOK FOR OUR FOUR FABULOUS MEN!

Each month some of today's bestselling authors bring
four new fabulous men to Harlequin American Romance.
Whether they're rebel ranchers, millionaire power brokers
or sexy single dads, they're all gallant princes—and
they're all ready to sweep you into lighthearted fantasies
and contemporary fairy tales where anything is possible
and where all your dreams come true!

You don't even have to make a wish...
Harlequin American Romance will grant your every desire!

Look for Harlequin American Romance
wherever Harlequin books are sold!